Ash

A novella in the
Wheels and Zombies series
M. Van

Ash

A novella in the
Wheels and Zombies series
M. Van

42Links Publishing

Visit:
www.42Links.net

Cover design by Shezaad Sudar
Edited by Book helpline

ISBN: 978-90-824472-2-4

1

The pumping beats pummeling my ears weren't enough to block out the annoying presence of, well, everyone. You might think people would be sympathetic to the sick, but no, they have to be bugged with needles, pain meds, or changing IVs. If it isn't the poking and prodding, it's the *are-you-okay* questions executed with just the right amount of false concern to haunt you until you eventually die.

Tammy walked around my bed to check a monitor and wrote something on her pad. Her oversized fish-eyes peered through a set of thick glasses that offset the rest of her appearance. If it weren't for those dreadful goggles, I'd bet she'd have a chance at a more exotic career than changing bedpans. She seemed to know it too. I had often seen her hunched over a little too far, leaving some good-looking smug a decent view of what her too-tight nurse's uniform had to offer. Yet she didn't do it for everyone. Over time, I noticed looks didn't matter that much, but deep pockets seemed a necessity. She wouldn't be the first nurse to search for riches among the dying.

Thank God, she wouldn't do that to me. Tammy wouldn't flash her boobs at a thirteen-year-old girl with a nearly bald, fuzzy head of hair and stage 4 cancer. The doctors figured I had a couple of months left, which sucked.

Tammy's mouth moved, and she gestured for me to remove the earplugs.

"I'll need that back in a while," she said, pointing a finger at the phone on my lap. "I'm running behind on my social calendar."

"Yeah, sure," I said as I took the plugs out. Tammy had been the only nurse nice enough to lend me her phone. I never made phone calls, but I liked to listen to music. The others must have been afraid I'd steal their property or make long distant calls. As if I had any means to run from this damn hospital with the spoils or know anyone to call except my social worker.

A botched lumbar puncture had left me paralyzed. So making a quick getaway wasn't on my resume anymore, not that I would ever steal from someone.

When Terrence entered, he passed the old geezers sharing my room without acknowledging them, as if looking at them would ruin his (in my opinion) too-cheap-to-wear-in-public suit. Not that the two old men could have noticed him. Old man Jarrod had come out of surgery that afternoon and was out cold. Gary had refused to die when the staff had removed his life support. The old man just lay in his bed, waiting for his heart to give up. Even his wife had stopped coming after a while.

Sweat plastered Terrence's forehead. He looked as if he had run up the five flights of stairs, but with a body about fifty pounds overweight, I figured even walking could mean a challenge for him. I followed his waddle across the room from the corner of my eye —the decision to ignore him made.

Terrence had become an obligatory visitor when they appointed him my caseworker. Besides failing miserably at his job because he still hadn't cleared up the mix-up that had put me in a room with these two old geezers and the strange odor that wafted around him, Terrence wasn't my favorite person in the world.

It wouldn't be long before they'd stick me in a box, so was it too much to ask for a room with people a little closer to my age? These old geezers were sixty and sixty-three years my senior. Never mind Gary, but the effects of Jarrod's Alzheimer's had started to get on my nerves.

Tammy entered the room as Terrence stopped at the foot of my bed. I used the phone to check the time and realized Tammy's shift was up. This screwed up my plan for ignoring Terrence.

"Sorry, girl," Tammy said. "I have to go." An annoyed sigh escaped me as I handed Tammy the phone.

"Thanks," I managed to say. Tammy hovered for a moment. As it brought forth the opportunity to ignore Terrence a little longer, I gave Tammy's fish eyes my full attention. Her mouth shifted into a thin line before her arms spread wide and surrounded me in a tight hug. I froze in shock—she must have lost it.

"Take care, girl," she said. As she let go, I looked at her, still in shock.

"I'll see you tomorrow—right?"

Tammy didn't answer my question. Her gaze shifted uneasily between Terrence and me. Terrence cocked his head with a motion to the door. Tammy took the hint and left with a slight wave of her hand. My eyes lingered on the door after Tammy had left, unsure of what had just happened.

The shift of metal over linoleum caught my attention. Terrence grabbed a chair from the far corner of the room and dragged it to the side of my bed to park his oversized butt on it. I glared at him incredulously. He had never taken the time to sit with me. A white handkerchief appeared in his hand from a pocket of his cheap suit. He daubed at the sweat on his forehead. He looked anxious.

"Listen, kid—" he started to say, but I stopped him before he could finish.

"I'm not a kid." My voice was firm and a bit loud, but I was sure my roommates wouldn't mind.

"Rebec—"

"Don't call me that either," I said in a harsh tone. Terrence cocked an eyebrow. "Call me Ash." My sister had come up with the nickname because of the color of my skin. She did it to annoy our parents, and it had become the only name I responded to. Terrence let out a deep sigh.

"All right, Ash," he said as if it cost him a tremendous amount of effort. "I'm leaving town tonight."

I shrugged without a reply. Why should I care if he left town?

"I should have known you'd be all heartbroken

about it," he said as he stood up from the chair. "I don't know when they're pulling you out but have a good life for what's left of it."

"Wait, what?" I said. "What do you mean, 'have a good life'? You're not comin' back?" The man is pretty much a douche, but a familiar one at least.

"Things are getting out of control," he said. "I have to get my family out of town."

"What things? And what did you mean, pull me out?" I asked. I heard about some riots, but what else is new?

"Haven't you watched the news? They're evacuating the city."

I blinked.

"They're evacuatin' Brooklyn," I said, more as a statement than a question. My words must have come out a little too cynical, because Terrence dropped his shoulders with emphasis.

"For a smart kid, you are pretty dense sometimes. The world did not stop moving because your life turned to shit; people are dying out there."

"Well, if you had done your job, Terrence, I might have had a television to watch. How the hell am I supposed to know what's goin' on out there? And don't call me kid." The words rushed out, the anger building inside me. Red spots broke out on Terrence's neck as his hands gripped my bed's railing.

"Well, maybe if you hadn't been such a foul-mouthed brat, I might have put some more effort into it," he said.

"As if my life is worth anythin' to write home

about," I said. "If I had a home." I could hear my voice break, and I hated it. I hated feeling sorry for myself. His grip on my bed relented, and the blood returned to his white knuckles.

"I don't have time for this. Figure it out." With that, he turned on his heels and stomped out of the room.

"Screw you," I shouted at his back, but he ignored me.

Except for the beeping and wheezing of machines that kept Gary and Jarrod alive, the room fell silent. My mind whirled at what had happened. Tammy's emotional goodbye, Terrence's, what, eviction notice? For a brief second, I wondered what douche the state would assign me next, but then Terrence's words started to filter in. He said they were evacuating the city, but how could that be and why? I needed to find out what was going on, but it had to wait until the night shift thinned out the staff. I rubbed a hand over the hair that barely covered my skull as my gaze shifted from the beds of the two old men to the window.

The orange glow of an invisible sun bounced off the window and reached my room. There was nothing to see but bricks and a sliver of blue sky fading into darkness.

I glanced at the legs hidden underneath the covers. They wouldn't even notice if a bus ran over them. That botched lumbar puncture that had left me paralyzed had been in the interest of my sister Alison's health. It wasn't so much the lumbar puncture, which as a procedure isn't supposed to be that invasive, but performed by a doctor on call for forty-eight hours with an appetite for synthetic drugs and alcohol, it had become a whole different ball game. He'd had a little trouble locating the lumbar vertebrae. The screw-up had left my parents busy with a potentially lucrative lawsuit, my sister depressed to the point of suicide, and me alone.

The only reason my parents even had me was to use me as a lab rat in an attempt to save Alison. I'd never blamed Alison—it hadn't been her fault she'd gotten sick. And she'd made it easy. Alison had been my favorite person in the world. I would have done anything for her. Instead, she had turned it around. For her, taking her own life had felt like the only thing she could do to set me free.

My parents had blamed me for Alison's death. It hadn't helped that her condition had turned out to be genetic, and I'd had the same thing. It had been the reason I hadn't been able to help her. My parents hadn't been able to handle it. After a while, they'd walked away from each other, and then from me.

| 2

The chair Terrence had left by my bed made it easier, but it was still a struggle to get to my wheelchair. When I had made from the bed to the chair, I slid to the ground. The nurses tended to make sure my wheelchair was well out of reach. They didn't like when I roamed the halls at night.

The linoleum felt clammy and sticky against my bare legs. The flimsy hospital gown they made me wear wasn't ideal for crawling around the floor, and what made it worse was that my naked butt stuck out. Refusing to think about it, I dragged my body across the room. My arms trembled with the effort. By the time I reached the wheelchair, my breaths came in hard and ragged. It took me a couple of minutes to regain my composure, and I managed to climb into the chair. Then I had to rest again.

There was nothing to tell the time by inside the room, but I wouldn't be surprised if that little trip from the bed to my chair had taken me thirty minutes. While I waited for my breathing to calm, I cursed the relentlessness of chemotherapy, then smoothed the thin fabric of my hospital gown over my legs, and set the chair in motion.

At the door, I stopped to listen, but the hall seemed empty. Most of the time, the night staff had waited around for a patient to ring the bell. That's when they'd jumped into action. The rest of their shift they had hovered around the lounge, watching television or playing cards.

I wheeled past the nurses' station, keeping my head low. The chair maneuvered almost soundlessly. I had gotten the hang of it this past year. This chair was the only thing besides some ragged jeans and a couple of sweatshirts that I actually owned. Well, Mom and Dad had paid for it, but that didn't prevent me from cherishing it. It kept me mobile, and it wasn't like those beat-up fifties' models provided by the hospital. I rolled past the open doors. With the lights off in most of the rooms, they looked like dark, gaping holes in the wall. Some of them had the bluish sheen of a television set that made me curse Terrence once again.

At the end of the hall, I pulled on the brake and whirled around the corner into the patients' break room without checking to see if one of the nurses had seen me go in. The wheels squeaked on the linoleum. Light from the television illuminated the room. I paused at the sight of smoke rising over the couch.

"Come on in," a broken voice with a heavy wheeze said. "I could use some company, watching the end of the world." I pushed my chair around the couch to face an old man, smoking a cigarette.

I glared at him. Not only was one not allowed to smoke in the hospital, but an air hose stuck up the old man's nose that looped around his ears before it drifted down to connect to a metal canister with a big "Flammable" sign on the side.

"Well, don't just sit there gawking. Come closer so

I can see you." A bit put off by the possibility of blowing up, I hesitated. Then I figured, what did I have to lose. As I rolled the chair closer, I noticed a woman fast asleep in the far-end corner of the room. I recognized her as one of the elderly ladies who spent their afternoons knitting around the television set. She'd been the one spreading all the new gossip while an IV filled her veins with some sort of liquid. The other chairs situated around the TV were empty.

"Don't mind her," the old man, who I had seen before but couldn't remember his name, said. "That old hag could never hold her liquor." Surprised, I saw that the old man held up a flask, saluted me, and chugged it down. The sight made me grin. The man might be old, but he surely knew how to entertain himself.

Light from the TV gave me a better view of him as he sat up. His head was almost square, and he had the air of a man who might have been tough as nails in his prime. White hair sat on his head with a touch of grease to keep it all slicked back. He reminded me of the gangsters from those old movies.

"You're a scrawny little thing, aren't you," he said. "How old are you?"

"Fifteen," I replied. The old man almost choked on his snorted laugh.

"You can't fool an old fool," he said, still coughing a laugh. "You don't look a year over ten."

"Thirteen," I said with a sigh. The old man smiled without the added throat noises.

"The name's Chuck," he said with a delighted

grin. The cigarette switched hands, and he held the empty one out to me.

"Ash," I said, and I couldn't help return the grin. He held my hand for a moment and peered at it as he shook his head.

"Thin as a feather," he said. "The one thing it doesn't do is discriminate, does it? God knows I've done my share of bad in my life and might even deserve my fate, but look at you." He shook his head again.

His gesture made me feel uncomfortable, and I turned away to inspect the floor. As if he noticed, he refrained from saying anything else.

He sat back with a sigh, followed by a nasty cough that made my stomach turn. When he regained control of his breathing, he gestured to the TV.

"We might have found our end in this," he said. The moisture in his eyes made me turn to watch the screen. What I saw on that screen made the blood drain from my face and hide in my toes.

An aerial shot made from a newscast helicopter showed a war zone in downtown Manhattan. Fires lit up the screen—buildings engulfed in flames. People scrambled up and down the streets. Fear rained down like a monsoon. At least, that's what I thought until the camera zoomed in. It wasn't fear that had overtaken these people—it was rage. They went at each other like rabid dogs.

The image switched to a pale-looking broadcaster. The sound on the set was too low for me to hear, but the expression on the man's face said plenty.

The news ticker at the bottom of the screen gave instructions for an evacuation. Then the screen changed to show buses driving off towards the highway. Military roadblocks denied any other vehicles the chance to reach those highways. Miles and miles of cars blocked every street and alleyway. People were desperate to get out of the city, but the military didn't allow anyone to leave without inspection.

"That takes the light right out of those pretty blue eyes of yours, doesn't it?" Chuck said. I gasped, unable to speak. Most of the carnage caused by a viral outbreak, according to the news ticker, was situated around the Manhattan area. However, they said it was spreading fast.

"What is this?" I said under my breath. Chuck eyed me curiously.

"You haven't seen this?" he asked. "This has been building for days."

I swallowed the lump in my throat. That's what Terrence meant when he told me off that the world hadn't stopped moving when my life turned to shit. I'd been so busy wallowing in my own misery, using music to cut myself off from the world, that I had missed this.

"I, eh …" I started to say, but my voice faded.

"I wonder how we'll get ourselves out of this one," Chuck mumbled under his breath.

We watched in silence when the old man wasn't coughing his lungs out. I lost track of time while I sat there, my eyes glued to the screen. A door clicked shut somewhere down the hall, and it pulled me out of my trance.

Chuck eyed me wearily and then said, "I'll tell you, half pint: this won't become any prettier." He extended his hand for me to shake. "Still, it was nice meeting you." He pointed a thumb at the door. "You better beat it before Nurse Ratched comes sniffing around."

I took his hand and shook it. For some reason, a feeling of finality hung in the air.

"Watch your back, half pint, and if I can help, you'll find me here, okay?"

"Okay," I said and tried a smile. It must have come out as a grimace because Chuck gave me a sympathetic look.

Thoughts swirled as I replayed the encounter with Chuck and the images from the TV in my mind. All of that was happening not far beyond these hospital walls. The information had hit me like a sledgehammer as I rolled my chair out of the break room. The hall looked empty past the door, and I risked it. The images on TV seemed to come straight out of a horror movie—one with terrifying special effects.

Besides fear, it invoked something else in me, something dark that hit me in an instant, and I felt complacent. *Why should I be the only one to suffer?* I bit my cheek to stop the thoughts in their tracks. It wouldn't do me any good to think like this. What happened to me wasn't anyone's fault, just plain bad luck, and if there was one thing Alison had taught me, it was not to hold grudges.

I neared the nurses' desk when the sound of rubber soles squeaking on the linoleum caught my attention. My chair's tires made a similar sound when I came to a halt. Silently cursing myself, I rolled into one of the dark holes in the wall. Three beds stood in the room, but none of the patients seemed awake. Peering out from the darkness, I watched Nurse Patterson stride past the open door. I knew she wouldn't be able to see me. The rooms were too dark.

Nurse Patterson had no lack of self-confidence. She was quite full of herself, with her dark hair neatly put up and pinned to her skull. Her nose always seemed to find its way up to the ceiling. I wondered if Chuck had meant her when he spoke of this Nurse Ratched. I didn't know any Nurse Ratched, but the name didn't sound very complimentary.

Careful to avoid making the wheels squeak, I peeked out and saw that at the end of the hall, Patterson took a left to enter the nurses' lounge. A breath escaped me. I needed to pass that lounge. Praying the uptight nurse had closed the door behind her, I edged closer. It seemed the luck that I had lacked ever since I had been born kept its consistency. The door stood wide open.

Voices whispered in the hallway, and I couldn't contain my curiosity. "When are they coming?" a voice that carried more tension than usually said. The voice belonged to Dr. O'Connell. I don't believe I had ever seen him at the hospital at this late hour.

Dr. O'Connell had established himself as a formidable healer over the years. His experience gave him seniority over most of the staff working at the hospital. He would have retired two years ago if they hadn't offered him a lucrative deal to stay on. His name and reputation had proven to work well in the market. Dr. O'Connell turned out to be modest enough to tell me that the moment we met. That's why it seemed odd to hear this strained voice coming from him. Although with everything going on outside, I guessed, even a seasoned doctor might start to show cracks.

Nurse Patterson, however, sounded as sure as always when she said, "Evacuation procedures for the patients start the day after tomorrow. A Captain Decker will be here bright and early tomorrow morning to start with the cancer wards. They won't be going to the safe zones."

"Why not? And why the special interest in the cancer wards?" O'Connell asked.

"I'm not sure. They wouldn't answer any of my questions, and frankly, I don't care. When I'm done tomorrow, I'm out of here."

"Where will you go?"

"I'm joining my sister's family. They're already up at one of the safe zones," Patterson said. "What's your plan?"

There was a moment of silence before O'Connell answered. I swear I could feel the tension build by the second even outside here in the hall.

"They'll never let me leave the island, so I can

forget about joining my daughter in California. I will try to stay with the patients—they'll appreciate a familiar face," he said. "I can't just hand them over to the military."

"Doctor, you're living in a dream world. Those patients will be part of some hush-hush research," Patterson said without hesitation. "You'll have to forget about them. No one is ever going to see them again."

My mouth dropped open at those last words. I recapped them in my mind, not sure if I had heard correctly, but they came back with exactly the same meaning. The military wanted to use the patients on the cancer ward as guinea pigs. The fact that I was part of that ward hit a second later. I gasped.

Footsteps lead into the hall. I scrambled to take off, but then I had to crane my neck to face the menacing eyes of Nurse Patterson. She gave me a look that made me feel as if the military coming to get me was the least of my problems.

"You nosy little brat," she said, stepping around and reaching for the handlebars of my chair. There wouldn't be much I could do, but I wouldn't let her get away with it easily.

"Hey, you can't touch my property," I said in a loud voice and rolled the chair backward. "Keep your hands off my chair." If looks could kill, I'd be dead.

"I'm going to do more than just touch your chair, you little piece of—" she started to say, but old man Chuck cut her off from where he stood in the door opening of the break room.

"You let half pint go, you Ratched," he called out from down the hall.

"I'll be coming for you next," Patterson shouted back. "Have you been smoking again? You old coot."

At that, voices started to complain from several rooms. Some shouted in Chuck's or my defense. Others just complained about the noise level. Patterson jerked at my chair as I tried to wrench away. I wanted to tell Chuck what I had heard, but I couldn't see any way to get to him.

"Nurse," O'Connell said in hushed yet stern voice, "please return Miss Reed to her room and quiet the rest." Patterson went for another pass at my chair. I couldn't see much choice but to give in.

3

The room was still on the dark side when I opened my eyes, but the white head of hair and the wheezing breath fed to him by a tube were unmistakable. Chuck stared at me wild-eyed.

"Well, see who finally decided to wake up," he said. I blinked in surprise at his figure hovering over my bed.

"What are you doin' in my room?"

"Never mind that. What did the old hag tell you last night?" he asked.

I looked at him in surprise and asked, "The old lady you gave an alcohol overdose?"

"No, half pint, the Ratched woman." Through a haze of half-sleep, I fought to recall the night before. My head felt so woozy that I wondered if Patterson had given me something to sleep, but I couldn't remember. I shook my head as if that would make it go away.

"She didn't tell me anythin', but I overheard her talk to O'Connell, and they spoke of evacuatin' patients—why?"

"Because I just saw half a dozen army vehicles with a bunch of buses pass my window and because my old friend Weaver—he's an old twat with a weak heart—admitted to cardiology two floors down," he said and then looked at me expectantly.

I didn't know the man with the weak heart, but I

nodded anyway to keep him talking.

"Well, he said that staff had been packing up for evacuation, but that shouldn't start until tomorrow."

"Ratched did mention that the evacuation of the patients would start tomorrow, but we're not gettin' evacuated," I blurted out. Chuck eyed me with furrowed brows. "That's what she said. They'll evacuate the rest of the hospital but not us—we're supposed to be taken someplace else." I pulled myself into a sitting position so I could face the old man.

"Why wouldn't they evacuate us?"

"I don't know, but Ratched—I mean, Patterson—said we'd be taken for hush-hush research, and they wouldn't have to deal with us anymore." My words came out high-pitched and a little frantic.

"Are you sure about that?" Chuck looked at me unconvinced.

"I'm not screwin' around here," I said as heavy boots fell outside the door. At the sound, Chuck's expression changed.

"Well, over my dead body," he said. I'd heard people say that before, but the look on Chuck's face told me he meant it. He strutted to the door, and I was afraid he would charge out. It would have looked impressive if he didn't have to drag that oxygen cart behind him and wasn't wearing a dreadful dark brown bathrobe. He stopped abruptly to ease open the door. Light that filtered through the crack made Jarrod grumble something incomprehensible in his sleep. Chuck poked his head out the door. As I waited in anticipation for what Chuck was about to do, I became very aware that my heart picked up speed. Chuck pulled his head back inside the room.

"Two men in green are chatting up O'Connell," he said in a hushed tone as he made his way to my bed.

"So," I said. Chuck ignored me. He frowned, which made the crinkles in his face reached new depths while he seemed deep in thought. When our gazes reconnected, Chuck's expression had changed. His eyes gleamed as if they had returned from the dead. A half-grin lifted his cheek into something devilish with a bit of charm. I raised my brows, not sure whether I liked where this was going.

"Where busting out of here, half pint." He said it in a slick, Jack Nicholson-from-*The Shining* tone of voice with a matching expression that felt a bit disconcerting. That movie, along with the book, stood high on my scare list, but that's what I liked about them. However, my expression must not have conveyed that, because Chuck's features softened.

"Come on, half pint. What have we got to lose?" he said as if he needed to convince me. "How long have they given you anyway?"

My throat clenched, and I had to swallow at that. Acknowledging that you're going to die and expressing an exact time frame seemed like a line I didn't want to cross. It would be too final.

Chuck, fortunately, didn't wait for an answer. "You want to spend those months in the hands of some Frankenstein?"

I shook my head, still uncertain of my voice.

"I mean, even if it is not that bad, you think they'll give a rat's ass how you spend your final days with all that going on outside?" He pointed a crooked finger at the window, reminding me of the chaos we'd seen on TV yesterday.

He was right of course. If what we had seen turned out to be spreading as fast as the news ticker had announced, the government would have their hands full. An image of an old World War II movie flashed in my head where they shipped off the sick and helpless to Nazi death camps. The thought made me shiver. Chuck watched me, waiting for my answer that in a way was easy, but on the other hand, wasn't.

I cleared my throat and said, "And how were you plannin' to get us out of here?" Relieved my voice had returned, I waved a hand over my legs to gesture at my mobility with a mock grin.

Chuck shrugged as if it were nothing before he crossed the room over to where my wheelchair stood in a corner. He maneuvered it awkwardly over to the bed, steering the chair with one hand and pulling the oxygen cart with the other. Without a word, he scooped me from the bed. Frail and too short for my age, I wouldn't be much of a challenge to carry anyway, and I could tell the old man, despite his bad smoking habit, had kept his body in shape over the years. He must have been one hulk of a man during his prime. He sat me in the chair, but then he lost his balance. He gripped the armrests, balancing his weight as he almost tipped us both over before regaining his footing.

"Sorry about that, half pint," he said, panting a little from the effort. I eyed him with a raised brow when he padded my near bald head. That would not have gone over well if it had been anyone else, but I could suffer it from the old man. At least, he didn't call me kid.

Despite the oxygen cart, Chuck moved with efficiency down the long white corridor of our hospital wing. I hovered at his back as much as I could in my chair on wheels. When necessary, we ducked into a darkened room at the sound of footsteps. Our wing treated severe cancer cases. Most patients hung on by threads, and at this early hour, it left us with an eerie silence only disturbed by the wheezing and beeping of respiration machines and heart monitors.

It changed when we neared one of the main junctions where three corridors converged. From around the corner, we could see that the evacuation of our special breed of patients had begun. The hospital had set this entire floor up as a dedicated cancer ward. I assumed this would make it a lot easier to haul us off in a relatively low-key fashion that wouldn't disturb the rest of the patients on other floors. Armed soldiers pushed beds from rooms and lined them up by the elevators. Nurses padded along the beds in an effort to keep the patients calm.

Disgruntled voices came from a sectioned-off portion at the beginning of the corridor. Several soldiers formed a line to keep a bunch of people separated from the patients. At least ten of them struggled with the soldiers for access. The soldiers wouldn't relent.

"They're family," Chuck said in a whisper. "I recognize Maggie's husband." I didn't recognize the woman's name or the man he pointed out down the hall. It must have shown on my face.

"You somewhat met yesterday," he said. "The old hag who had trouble holding down the booze."

I nodded absentmindedly, a bit on edge from the violent shouts flaring from the corner where soldiers held back the family members.

"How would they know to come so early?" I asked in a hushed voice.

"Who knows these days," Chuck said, "with all these handheld boxes you kids play with …" His throat made a wheezy sound, and he cupped a hand over his mouth. After some disgusting gurgling sounds, he continued. "Anyone could have called them."

When I peered around the corner, I witnessed Maggie's husband, a little fat guy with greasy hair, shove one of the soldiers in the shoulders. The soldier didn't even flinch. It didn't stop another soldier from shoving the little fat man in return. Maggie's husband stumbled backward into some other family members. An entangled mess of arms couldn't stop him from falling on his butt.

A feisty redhead who had witnessed it slapped the soldier in his face. He, in turn, shoved the redhead as he had Maggie's husband. The redheaded woman barely took a step back, but she cried out in anger. A burly man reacted and punched the soldier square in the face.

The situation escalated like a brushfire. This was our chance. I yanked on Chuck's ugly bathrobe. He looked down at me over his shoulder and then followed my finger to where it pointed across the hall to a pair of elevators. The grin on his face told me he was thinking the same thing. Chuck took another peek around the corner while I watched his hand extended in a gesture not to move. I could feel the adrenaline rise in anticipation, my hands poised on the wheels, ready to haul ass. Chuck's hand twitched. I went. Wheels spun fast as I hurried to the elevator doors. With ease, I came to a halt, spun the chair, and hit the button in one quick action. I had just motioned to Chuck, who had made it halfway, to hurry up when a figure in green stepped around the corner.

"Hold on. Where are you two going off to?" a female voice said.

Chuck stopped in his tracks, his eyes closed, face set in a grimace that carved deep crevices into his wrinkled skin. Holding my breath, I watched the woman step closer.

Over her green uniform, she wore an armored vest, a gun holstered at her side, and an assault rifle strung across her chest. She didn't stand tall in her army-issued boots, but the dark, braided hair molded into a Mohawk at the top made her look impressive. She stopped next to Chuck and placed a tentative hand on his shoulder. I would have expected her to pull a gun or start shouting for the others. Instead, she let out a breath, and her dark eyes filled with concern.

"You must be Miss Reed," she said in a soft tone as she released Chuck's shoulder. "Nurse Patterson said you might have figured out a thing or two, and I see you've enlisted a friend."

Chuck folded his arms over his chest and rested his butt against an empty bed that someone had parked in the hall. He eyed the woman suspiciously.

The elevator next to me dinged, and the doors whooshed open. A tall man in uniform stepped out. His dark skin jumped out against the white walls and tiled floor. He looked down at me with a smile that reached his blazing jade-green eyes.

"Sergeant," he said when he turned to the Mohawk woman.

"Lieutenant," she replied.

"Everything all right?"

"Yes, sir," she said. "I was just escorting these two for a bathroom break."

"I see," the lieutenant replied. "Carry on." With a nod, the lieutenant walked off in the direction of the violent shouts that seemed to have increased.

With the lieutenant's back turned to us, I glared at the sergeant with wide eyes. Chuck shifted his gaze between the both us looking confused. The sergeant placed her hands on her hips and shook her head.

"This is so fucked up," she muttered under her breath.

"You can start by letting us onto this elevator,"

Chuck said, seizing the opportunity at the sergeant's hesitation.

"I'm sorry, I can't let you sneak off. Besides, they'll comb out the hospital if I don't bring you back," she said. She looked from Chuck to me and then over her shoulder to where the shouts came from around the corner. "The fact that we don't agree with our orders probably won't be much of a comfort."

"Why are they doing this?" I asked. She angled her head down to face me.

"Someone figured that cancer might provide a cure for that rabies virus that is destroying the city."

"So it's true what half pint said. They will experiment on us and shove us in cages like rats," Chuck said and took a step back.

Feeling sick to my stomach, I swallowed hard to shove the bile down. A shiver ran down my body at the same time the color drained from my face. Doctors had poked and prodded me my entire life. This wasn't right. This couldn't be happening. I took hold of my stomach, unable to stop the bile rising in my throat and threw up over the armrest of my chair. The white tiled floor turned a disgusting yellow.

The sergeant kneeled beside me as I wiped my mouth with the collar of my hospital gown.

"I'm so sorry, kid," she said, her hand on mine. Her words triggered a spark of anger. I jerked from her grasp and rolled the wheelchair out of her reach.

"I'm not a kid, and I'm not going to be your lab rat," I said caustically. I could see the hurt in her eyes, the trouble she had with what she was supposed to do, but it didn't mean she wouldn't.

The sergeant got to her feet and shot a glance over her shoulder as the noises reached a new level. A gunshot rang out.

4

Shouts, screams, and gunfire erupted from around the corner. The sergeant gripped her rifle and had it pointed at the end of the hallway in an instance. A body, dressed in a similar style as the sergeant, flung itself around the corner, stumbling to the ground. On hands and feet, the soldier struggled to get upright. Another body cornered the hall, walking backward with careful steps, his back turned to us, his rifle firing short bursts. Shooters with a constant finger on their trigger remained unseen, but the violent rat-tat-tat of automatic machine gunfire alerted us to their presence. Something had the soldiers on the defense, and I couldn't believe it to be the family members.

That first soldier came running at us, shouting the sergeant's name. "Sergeant Meadow, they're here, they're here!" The fear in the young man's voice didn't fit with the assault gear he carried.

"Calm down, Burke," Sergeant Meadow called out over the man's whining.

The second soldier pulled his rifle from around the corner when a body slid across the linoleum and slammed into the wall. Blood smeared where the body had left a track. A ragged-looking figure jumped the lifeless form and started ripping with its teeth at the dead man's clothes. The figure growled in frustration when it couldn't get through the layers of clothes. My mouth gaped at the rage that poured from the man and the blood that ran down his mouth.

The second soldier retreated to us, reloading his gun when two more figures came into view. I gasped at the sight. Along with the man still tearing at the dead man's clothes, these two new figures looked like the scrambling people in the streets of Manhattan that I had seen in the broadcast.

"Get down," Sergeant Meadow shouted. She fired several shots after the two approaching soldiers ducked to a side. "Not-a-kid-"—she nodded at the elevator—"press the down button, will ya?"

I looked at her, confused, but I did as she asked. Everything inside screamed for me to turn around and roll my chair as fast as I could to get away from the sergeant and her band of gunslingers, but what good would that do me?

Additional figures strode into our hallway. Among them, I spotted Maggie's husband with his short, bulky features. Blood covered his white shirt. He drew his nose into the air and stretched his mouth wide open. His nostrils flared as he sucked in air. Followed by several others, he came running at us at an impressive speed for a man his size.

The second soldier had managed to reload his weapon. He turned to fire several bursts of bullets, followed by the report of Sergeant Meadow's rifle. Burke skidded to a stop in front of me and then shoved my chair back.

"Hey," I yelled at him. Franticly, he started to jab at the elevator buttons.

"Come on, come on," he repeated under his breath. I maneuvered my chair so I could glance around the chanting soldier.

Bullets fired by the second soldier tore into a woman's chest. Her body jerked, and her pink nurse's uniform turned red in places where the bullets had struck. Except for the hair put up and pinned to her skull, not much of the self-confident woman who used to be Nurse Patterson remained. Her eyes nearly bulged out of her head, and a white, milky film swam across her irises. Like all the raging people hurtling for us from the end of the hall, she too had those creepy white eyes. I gripped the armrest so hard that the muscles in my arms started to protest. Nurse Patterson had been a nuisance over the years, but now she just scared me.

Bam, bam, Nurse Patterson's head splashed open in a haze of blood.

"Go for the head, Jonesy," Sergeant Meadow said. The second soldier, apparently called Jonesy nodded.

Even more crazy-acting people filled up the hall, cramming into the space like sardines in a can. They didn't seem to have any concern for their own well-being as they slammed into beds that stood as hurdles in their path while others trampled over the fallen bodies.

Jonesy fired several more shots before the elevator dinged.

"Thank God," Burke said, clawing at the doors to help them open faster. With that, he nearly knocked me over by bumping into me. Before I could curse him to hell and back, Chuck grabbed his collar and slammed him against the wall.

"Listen, you little piece shit," he said. "If you touch that girl one more time, I will rip your throat out myself." Blood drained from Burke's face.

"God dammit, Burke. Get a grip. You're supposed to be a soldier," Sergeant Meadow shouted at the man.

Chuck half shoved, half threw Burke inside the elevator box. Chuck breathed hard as his hand gripped the railing of one of the abandoned empty beds that cluttered the hallway. He looked at me in concern. I could only grin up at the man. The exertion had knocked the wind out of him, and he relied heavily on the oxygen provided by the cart, but in my book, he was awesome.

Jonesy ushered my chair inside after Chuck, and Sergeant Meadow crammed in last. She kept firing her rifle until the doors closed. When motion set in, she hit the emergency stop.

Her eyes went around the box after she had reloaded her weapon, eyeing each of us for just a moment. She stopped with Burke and said, "What the hell happened back there?"

The man started rattling incomprehensible sentences that might have made sense to a ten-month-old. Meadow slapped him in the face.

"Is he on drugs or something?" she asked Jonesy. Jonesy shrugged in return. The slap seemed to have calmed Burke down, and he slumped against the wall.

"Anyone mind telling me what happened?" Meadow said in an unamused tone.

"One of the elevators on the south side opened, and a bunch of infected swarmed out where we had placed the families," Jonesy said. "We were cut off from the rest and bolted."

Meadow took a deep breath before she spoke. "We have to assume the hospital is compromised. Is underground parking still our rendezvous point?" Jonesy nodded.

"Anyone have a radio?" she asked. Both men eyed each other for a moment before their gazes dropped to the floor. Sergeant Meadow didn't berate the men for not having radios, probably because she didn't have one herself.

She continued. "Okay, we're heading down. Without contact, we won't know what we'll find …" She paused for a second to look at Chuck and me. "You two stay back. We'll take the lead."

Chuck cocked his head and glanced sideways at Burke.

"Sure …" Burke said elongating the word, confirming to be the ten-month-old I'd thought him to be. The three soldiers maneuvered to the front as Meadow released the emergency stop.

Agonizingly slow, the digital numbers counted down. The woman and the two men stood tall, weapons raised, ready to pounce. Well, at least, two of them did. Burke looked as if he was about to soil himself. The elevator descended while the tension in the tiny room rose. The low hum of the elevator did nothing to cover the sound of my pounding heart. At the touch of Chuck's hand on my shoulder, I looked up. His mouth curved in to a comforting smile unobscured by his wrinkled face.

"Don't worry, half pint. It'll be okay," he said. I managed to smile, but I didn't feel okay. My stomach churned, and the taste of bile remained at the back of my throat. My body felt tired, and I longed for my bed. I couldn't wrap my head around the fact that we were actually on the run from people gone crazy. The rage reflected upon those people's faces scared me.

The number changed again as I eyed the door. It wouldn't matter what we found beyond that elevator door—it would be all bad. If the ground floor turned out to be empty, these soldiers would roll us out and load us onto a bus. If the room ended up filled with crazies, we would likely die inside this box. It made me wonder what was worse. *Death by a crazy person or death by needle poking?*

I held my breath when the elevator came to a stop and dinged. The soldiers tightened their grips on their rifles as the doors slid open.

It seemed I had gotten my wish. The elevator revealed a partial view of the main entry to the hospital. The open space purposely designed with a lot of windows showed the start of a bright sunny day. I could see parts of the maroon-colored seating areas and an information desk decorated in that same hideous color. I imagined I would have been able to see the massive revolving doors or grainy pillars that held up the second-floor balcony, but it all remained obscured, blocked by dozens of legs. Sitting in my chair limited my view, but I had always been on the short side. It had its perks.

With a little pout on my face, I would usually be able to get what I wanted. Like the last day I spent with my sister. She had snuck us out, and we'd gone to a movie theater, except we had forgotten to bring any money. That little pout had gone a long way with the ticket officer. Combined with my tiny stature in an oversized wheelchair, my sister's bald head—my hair was still a long blond, nearly white—it hadn't taken much to convince the man to let us in without paying. We'd even managed two Cokes and a large tub of popcorn. The only problem had been that because I looked like a nine-year-old, we'd had to sit through a Disney movie. But that didn't matter, I had a blast.

It took a second for the crazies to react, but then a couple of them stuck their noses in the air. Nostrils flared, and as if synchronized, their gazes shifted to the open door. They looked ominous, with their foggy white eyes, shuffling from foot to foot. Some of them had lacerations on their faces and arms. Blood had spread on their clothes like ink stains. Mouths opened slowly, as if in slow motion, to stretch out wide, and then they surged for the open doors. *For us!*

Meadow was already slamming the button, but it seemed to take forever for the elevator doors to close. Jonesy fired his weapon, bam, bam, bam, and bodies slumped to the ground. My eyes widened at the outstretched arms and bony fingers that reached for us. Every time one of them came too close, Meadow or Jonesy would fire a couple of rounds. Even Burke managed to get in a shot or two. Blood along with brain matter sprayed the room, and the white and maroon patterns of the tiled floor became a dark, almost black, crimson.

Chuck tightened his grip on my shoulder. My hands gripped the wheels of my chair as if my life depended on it. *Maybe being eaten by the crazies wasn't such a good idea after all.*

Finally, the doors started to close. A mutilated face with a soggy hole for an eye tried to follow us. Before it actually reached the doors, Jonesy carelessly placed his handgun in the center of its head and pulled the trigger. The head snapped back. Jonesy jerked his hand back inside the elevator and the doors closed.

As soon as the elevator had lifted from the ground, Meadow slammed the emergency brake. "Everyone all right?" she asked, glancing around the box.

"Just peachy," Chuck said between wheezy breaths. I released the breath I was holding, and nodded. Burke repeated a frantic "yeah, yeah, yeah," and Jonesy shrugged. Apparently, he wasn't a man of many words.

Meadow checked her weapon. For a brief moment, her eyes went to the row of buttons indicating the available floors, and I guessed she must have noticed the lack of sublevel buttons.

"I suppose we won't be able to get to the parking

garage in this box?" she said.

"Nope," Jonesy replied.

"Suggestions," Meadow said. "Anyone know the layout of this place?" The soldiers looked at each other, but none of them answered. I raised a trembling hand.

"I know my way around."

Chuck included, everyone inside the elevator looked at me as if I had something nasty up my nose. Meadow managed to kneel down in the tight space.

"I used to sneak out of here with my sister," I added. She narrowed her eyes at me. Her expression showed doubt, and why wouldn't she doubt me? In her eyes, I was only a kid in a wheelchair.

Still, I was surprised to hear her say, "What's on your mind, not-a-kid?" I bit my lip to stifle a grin.

"Call me Ash," I said.

Meadow looked up at the other three. "We're close enough to smell each other. I guess introductions are in order." She held her hand out.

"Angie," she said when I took her hand to shake it. She pointed out the other men. "Private Taylor Burke and Private First Class Xander Jones."

Jonesy held out his hand and said, "With an X, but call me Jonesy." He had a clean-shaven face, and his grin showed a row of white teeth. Most of his face remained hidden behind dark shades and a helmet, although the expression on his mouth looked sincere.

Chuck introduced himself as Charles West, but he preferred Chuck. Burke just about squeaked his own name when Chuck offered to shake his hand. It could be just me, but it looked like Burke felt a little intimidated by Chuck. This wasn't a surprise, remembering the way Chuck had slammed him into the wall.

"Okay, introductions made, let's hear it, Ash," Angie said. The fact she was willing to hear me out without dismissing me as a little kid boosted my confidence and raised my opinion of her. I had to remind myself that she had an agenda, and it wasn't just to get us out. It was to hand Chuck and me over to some military lab. The fact that I started to like her shouldn't make me less cautious.

With tightness in my chest, I started to explain. I wasn't eager to tell them that only the elevators closest to the entry in the main hall reached the sublevel parking garage, but that we could take the stairs. Those stairs went up to the second floor, so we didn't have to get to them through the main hall.

"We could go up to the second floor, find the stairs, and then make our way down to the sublevel. It shouldn't be too hard..." I said, but trailed off as I thought about it. The stairs probably had fewer crazies, but it would also mean that we'd meet up with the rest of the military convoy ready to take us God knows where, to do God knows what.

"Second floor, it is," Angie said.

5

The elevator door dinged and opened with a whoosh. As before, the soldiers stood ready with their guns, but as far as we could see through the opening, the coast looked clear. Jonesy took point and veered to the left. Burke, who seemed to have reclaimed his composure, took the right. Angie hung back with Chuck and me.

"Mr. West—" she started to say, but Chuck cut her off.

"It's Chuck, sweetheart," he said. The old coot managed it with such flare that it made Angie blush. She cleared her throat.

"Chuck, I would like you to stick with Ash." She pulled the handgun from her holster and handed it to the old man. "Don't show it to the others if you don't have to, but don't hesitate to use it on the infected, even if they tend to act differently."

I gaped at the exchange. I imagined it was a risk for Angie to hand her gun to a stranger. It made me like her a whole lot more. Chuck cocked his head when he took the gun.

"What do you mean, act strangely?" he asked. Angie let out a breath.

"You'll see soon enough." With a glance over her shoulder, she stepped out of the elevator and followed Jonesy. Chuck looked down at me with a smile.

"I like her," he said while he pocketed the gun in

his ugly brown robe.

Chuck hooked his oxygen cart onto the back of my chair and pushed me out of the elevator.

"I can do it myself," I said, trying to keep the annoyance out of my voice.

"Sergeant Meadow ordered me to stick to you, and that's what I'll do," he replied. "I've never been one to defy orders."

"Don't tell me you're one of these military types."

"I might have been a private once," Chuck answered. I looked up at his wrinkled face and shook my head.

The door to the elevator had opened into a short hallway that would lead to the second-floor balcony. The balcony rounded above the entire main entry. I used to like sitting there, watching the people bustling below. A lot of them would be visiting a friend or family member who'd been admitted. On some you could see the tension in their shoulders as they sat down with a cup of coffee in the seating areas, waiting for news brought by some doctor. Even from up on the balcony, I could sometimes sense their fear and feel their relief when the doctor would bring good news.

From my visits, I knew the balcony merged with several side corridors, providing access to the different parts of the hospital and, of course, the staircase that would lead down to the sublevel parking garage. Frosted-glass doors at the end of the short hall denied us a view of the balcony itself and the marked exit doors.

Angie pointed to a seating area that wasn't more than a bunch of plastic chairs bolted to the wall.

"You stay put. I'll check it out," she said in a whisper.

Chuck seemed grateful at a chance to sit, and he unhooked his cart from my chair. I scooted close to him while Jonesy kneeled nearby, his gun at the ready. Angie shot Burke a look that even I could tell meant he'd better not fuck up before she turned on her heels and set off in the direction of the frosted-glass doors.

I watched her ease open the doors and poke her head through. A moment later she was out of sight. That seemed to unnerve Burke because he started pacing the short hallway. Jonesy popped a strip of chewing gum into his mouth. He offered Chuck and me a piece, but we both declined. He kept a wary eye on Burke while he scanned the area.

Every other second I threw an anxious glance at the frosted-glass doors. I guessed Angie's departure had put me off balance me as much as it had Burke. I took comfort in her ability to maintain a level head, and I liked her for not dismissing me as just a kid. It screwed with my head that on one weird level: I trusted her with my life, though I knew she'd put me on a bus the minute this was over.

"You doing okay there, Ash?" Jonesy's voice pulled me out of my haze of thoughts. I couldn't read the expression behind his shades, but I wouldn't have been surprised if he thought I was losing it.

"Yeah, fine," I replied.

"Half pint here is tough as nails," Chuck commented. I returned a half-smile.

"Why do you call her half pint?" Jonesy asked. Maybe he wanted to lighten the mood.

"Ah," Chuck started, "my grandson always resented it when I called him kid." A smile lit up Chuck's face at the memory of his grandson. "Kept telling me he wasn't a kid by the time he was ten. One day his mother sent him to pull me out of a bar, and the name somehow came to be."

Tears welled up in the old man's eyes. For the first time, I noticed they were a soft gray.

"Where is he now?" I asked.

"His mother refused to let me see him when he was still a boy. She was right, too—nobody likes a drunk," he said as if the words weighed him down. "But he came to see me a few months ago, him and his little boy. He called him Charley." The old man's face brightened for an instance, but then simmered down into a frown.

"He and the rest of his family live up in Canada," Chuck added with a deep sigh. "Perhaps things aren't as bad up there."

"I'm sure they're not," Jonesy said. "We have gotten the worst down here where it started."

Chuck nodded but diverted his eyes to the floor.

"Listen to him," I said, placing a hand on Chuck's arm. "Jonesy's been out there; he knows."

Footsteps came up from behind me. I had almost forgotten about Burke.

"You don't get it, do you?" Burke exclaimed.

"This thing is going to eat the world, and we're babysitting some goddamn Hail Mary."

"Shut up, Burke, and take your post," Jonesy said. Burke paced up and down the hall.

"I have to get out of here," Burke said, clamping his rifle to his chest.

"Just calm down, son," Chuck said. But it was as if Burke wasn't there anymore. He stared straight through us as if he had X-ray vision.

"Burke," Jonesy said with a wary undertone.

Burke spun on his heel and walked off to the end of the hall. He raised his rifle to his chest and peered around the corner. Jonesy got to his feet as he shot us a worried glance. At least, I think it meant worried. Those shades started to unsettle me. He followed Burke a few paces but stopped when Burke stepped around the corner and out of sight. His fast-paced footsteps echoed back to us as he sprinted down the hall.

"Burke," Jonesy called out in a low voice.

"Shouldn't you go after him?" I asked as he watched Burke run down the hall. Jonesy shook his head.

"He made his choice."

We waited in silence for a couple of minutes until the frosted-glass doors opened, and Angie reappeared. She shook her head at Jonesy and then stopped in surprise. She lifted her shoulders and dipped her head, clearly wondering where Burke had run off. Jonesy shook his head with a shrug. The gesture seemed to explain all, because from her expression, I could read the curse words singing around in her head.

"Stupid idiot," she muttered when she neared us and kneeled next to my chair. "That way is blocked. The place is crawling with infected."

Without another word, they all looked at me. My eyes widened, and I had to swallow hard. All my nightly excursions ran inside my mind. I knew this hospital like the back of my hands. I'd practically lived in this place for most of my life, but now I had trouble remembering.

My chest tightened at the expectant glances, and I had trouble sucking in air. Chuck's nostril plugs caught my eye. I wondered if I could borrow them to release the strain on my lungs as an image of my sister smiling in the sunlight rammed into my thoughts.

"I know a way," I said with a gasp. Relief washed over me when their worried expressions changed into half-smiles. Angie's face lit up even more when I told her about a maintenance exit I had used sneaking out with my sister. It let out into a small courtyard that connected to the hospital grounds.

My sister and I had used it once to sneak out after some bad procedure had left her in tears. She was too exhausted to get very far, but a patch of grass and the sun on her face had done the trick to change her mood.

Chuck had gotten to his feet. We were ready to move when we heard footsteps stomping down the hall. Incoherent screams followed when Burke's form spun around the corner where it came to a halt. Wild eyes shot from Angie to the door and back. They went even wider when he said, "You're back. It's clear." He sounded like that ten-month-old again, and then he sprinted to the door.

"Don't," Angie shouted. Jonesy tried to tackle him, but Burke was too fast, and he slammed his body into the frosted glass. With a crack, one of the doors splintered in several places. In shock, I peered past the opened doors. Crazies stood shoulder to shoulder and packed the room.

Growls erupted from the room, along with a high-pitched scream that had to have come from Burke as the crazies piled on top of him. I looked at Angie in search of answers—how had she been able to get out of there? But there was no time. The growls didn't stop when the screams died, and the open door gave the crazies an excellent view of the four of us.

"Go, go, go," Angie said as she ushered us to move. "Jonesy, help Chuck. Ash, you're driving on your own. I'll take the rear." With that, she spun and fired several shots.

Jonesy had one of Chuck's arms draped around his shoulders. He forced the old man to a quicker pace. In my chair, I could have been faster, but I decided to stay behind them. What I saw at the corner of the short hallway would have knocked me off my feet if I'd been able to stand.

An army of crazies had followed Burke. That's why he had come charging around that corner like an idiot, and now he had led them straight to us. They plowed down the hall in a parade of snarls and snapping jaws, in a variation of hospital gowns, doctors' coats, and pink nurses' outfits, combined with a mixture of blood and gore.

Jonesy stopped in the middle of the junction and fired his rifle, one-handed. Chuck didn't hesitate as he pulled the handgun that Angie had given him from the pocket of his bathrobe and fired.

"Angie," I shouted when I had lost sight of her in the confusion. Fear of the oncoming horde made my heart pound in overdrive. I didn't think I could stand if we lost another one of our little group, and I felt relieved when I heard her voice. I would probably never say it out loud because of my own damn pride to admit it, but I needed them.

"Move," she retorted and took Jonesy's place. Her rifle fired in quick succession as I rolled my chair to follow in Jonesy and Chuck's footsteps. I chanced a glance behind me. Angie had managed to stop the advance.

Bodies lay in heaps of entangled arms and legs, which gave the ones still upright trouble enough to follow us. Jonesy gave Chuck quite the exercise. They had made it around the corner and vanished from sight. I hurried after them, spinning my wheels as fast as I could, almost bumping into them.

"Where do we go, Ash?" Jonesy asked. He glanced down the hall that looked the same as the one we had just come from.

A combination of loud, clustered gunfire made me jump. A handful of lumbering bodies fell to the ground. Jonesy kept his weapon at the ready as he stepped into the hall with the grayish-white linoleum floor. Along with the floor, the white walls with a yellow finish now had a dark red almost black splatter pattern where the bodies had crumpled to the ground and drenched in their own blood.

Every dozen feet or so, there was a door, some open, some closed. About halfway down the hall, I made out a reception area for this specific ward. At the end of the long hall, I spotted what I was looking for.

"There," I said pointing it out. "That red door on the left." Without hesitation, the men sprang into motion. Footsteps alerted me to Angie's approach, and I rolled my chair back to peer into the hallway we had come from.

"We found it," I said, unable to hide my enthusiasm. I instantly registered my reaction as stupid. I read it in the smile that wouldn't reach her eyes. I wasn't helping myself here, or Chuck, but what was I supposed to do, let us all get killed by a bunch of bloodthirsty, infected crazies?

"Go," Angie said, with a hand on my shoulder. Then she spoke louder so Jonesy would hear. "Don't you stop for anything. You hear me? Get them out."

With my wheels in motion, I glanced back as Angie fired the first shot. The crazies must have gotten past the barricade of fallen bodies.

Jonesy and Chuck reached the door, but they seemed to have trouble getting it open. Jonesy inspected the door for a second while the repetition of gunfire behind us increased. I glanced over my shoulder and saw a few had already breached the corners. A body crumpled to the ground with every shot, but with every mutilated figure that went down, another took its place. They started to push Angie into retreat.

"Son," Chuck said impatiently, with an eye on the crazies that were forcing Angie back to us with every second.

Jonesy glanced up with a smirk, and then without a word, he lifted his boot and kicked in the door. A brief smile lifted the corners of my mouth when the door opened with a crack, until I heard the click, click of an empty rifle.

6

When I turned, Angie had disappeared. A pack of dazed-looking crazies milled around the hall we had come from, just beyond the information desk area. They seemed lost as they stumbled and crawled like drunks around the fallen bodies. Without thinking, I pushed my chair forward. I heard Chuck call out my name, followed by several footsteps, but I picked up speed quickly. I almost made it to the reception area when my common sense kicked in. What the hell was I doing? I didn't have a weapon, and I wasn't exactly the right person to help Angie. All of a sudden, I remembered Angie didn't have her backup weapon. She'd given it to Chuck, and her rifle had clicked empty. I swallowed hard when the crazies who were mere feet from the reception area found something interesting rolling toward them and charged.

I couldn't make it, not without being shredded to pieces. White foggy eyes had set their sights on me. Fingers clutched the air. Carcasses of human bodies moved in a shuffle of the dead, pulling and tugging at each other. My heart pounded in my chest while I shouted Angie's name. She didn't answer. Shredded to pieces by bullets, bodies littered the ground in front of the reception desk. I pulled on the brakes, and I came to a stop before I reached the desk. There were no green army fatigues visible on the floor, but I couldn't waste time searching—I had to get out of there. Pushing down a vast range of emotions that threatened to spill from my eyes, I turned. Through blurred vision, I noticed Jonesy and Chuck had disappeared from the hall. *Couldn't they have waited for one damn minute?*

I pushed the wheels, setting the chair in motion. Deep-rooted, gut-wrenching sounds closed in on me. I fought to speed up when my chair jerked to a stop. *What the hell!* I looked down to see that one of the crazies who I had thought to be dead by Angie's hand had stuffed his arm between the spokes of my wheel. Its body lay limp on the floor, but its head perked up. A woman, who must have been beautiful at one time, eyed me with half of her face missing. I screamed.

With frantic tugs on the wheel, I tried to wrench free, but the arm wouldn't budge. Over my shoulder, I saw others right on top of me. Two limped by as if they hadn't seen me. A man in a green uniform lunged for the chair. I leaned forward and dropped myself out of the seat. My chin connected hard with the linoleum floor. The infected soldier came crashing to the floor with my chair. I scrambled on my arms to get away before he crushed me, or worse, ate me. The soldier crawled after me. The rifle still hung across its chest. Lucky for me, the rifle made its movements even more awkward. I gripped a doorpost to get some leverage, but it was no use—I couldn't get away from the man. My arm lifted, as if that would be any kind of defense. When I felt its awful breath on my arm, I screamed my throat raw.

Something yanked the crazy off me, and its face

smacked against the ground. Through teary eyes, I saw Angie lift her arms and smash the butt of her rifle into the crazy's head. The head cracked open. A second later, Angie was on me, and she lifted me off the floor. She dragged me into a room and slammed the door shut. We both slumped to the ground, breathing heavily.

"That was a stupid thing to do, kid," Angie whispered near my ear. My heart had stopped and restarted with a jolt. It felt as if it wanted to jump out of my chest.

"I'm not a kid," I said in a low whisper between breaths.

"As long as you act like one, you are one, kid." Ready to chastise Angie, I turned, but a finger covered her lips before it pointed to the door. I followed its direction and gasped. A shadow passed the light where it filtered in underneath the door slit. As it shuffled by, I felt Angie's body relax. I took the moment to take in our surroundings.

Fortunately, the patient's room we had entered sat empty. Another one of the crazies shambled past the door. Its shadow stopped, followed by a muffled moan. My body pressed into Angie.

"It's okay," she whispered. "They won't bother us once they have calmed down."

I looked up at her dumbfounded, and nothing more than a "Huh" fell from my mouth.

"Cancer perk," she said. I blinked. A smile that for the first time reached her eyes spread across her face. "People like us have to find the positive in the little things." Before I could demand an explanation, she got to her knee and peeked out the door.

A man in a hospital gown stood near the door opening. Dark red splotches ran from his mouth down to his gown. A bloodied hand had a firm grip on an IV drip while he stood shuffling from foot to foot. Several others passed the door, and after a moment, the one in our door opening followed. Ignoring them, Angie stepped out, righted my chair, and rolled it into the room before closing the door behind her.

When she had me seated in my chair, she dropped down on the bed. I crossed my arms and narrowed my eyes at her, ready for some answers. A crooked smile lifted her mouth to one side, taking some of that hard focus away from her eyes, which in the dim room almost looked black. She leaned back on her hands, and the smile disappeared.

"The infected don't eat cancer patients. They might attack if they're agitated, but usually don't," she said. "It's something in the makeup of the cells that doesn't compute with the virus."

My eyes widened at her admission. Mouth open, I glared at her. When I had collected my thoughts, I managed to speak again. "But they ignored you as well, just now, and back there on the balcony."

Angie sat up and shifted uncomfortably on the bed.

"I went in for an annual checkup about two weeks ago. It didn't pan out that well," she said as her gaze shifted from me to the floor. "It was quite a shock. I'd been cancer free for over ten years, so …" Her voice drifted off.

I wanted to feel sorry for her, but her reason for being here kept me from doing so. My hands gripped the wheels on my side so tight that my knuckles went white. Between gritted teeth I said, "They don't know." She shook her head, diverting her eyes again.

"I was going to tell them, but then this happened."

"And now you're collecting their lab rats while you're supposed to be one yourself," I said. I couldn't withhold the venomous tone, but I managed not to spit on her.

"It's more complicated than that, I …" She looked at me and then cut herself off as if she decided I wasn't worth the explanation. My temper flared.

"You bitch," I said. The crazies stirred outside the door at the sound of my loud voice, but I didn't care. My whole body shook in anger, and my nostrils flared to accommodate the extra air I needed to circulate the rage pumping through my veins. I had come to admire her bravery, but she was just a backstabbing coward to save her own ass. "You're just a coward."

"What would you want me to do, huh? Tell them, 'Hi, here I am, you forgot one'?" she said as her arms went up to make her point. "'Now cut me open like a fish.'" She slid from the bed and bent down to face me. "Is that what you want me to do?"

Her eyes bore into mine as she spoke in a low tone that barely reached a whisper while she shredded my resolve. She was right; it wasn't that simple. My eyes dropped to my hands where I had folded them in my lap.

"You could have left," I said in a whisper.

"That's the complicated part."

I looked up at her, but she shook her head and stood up straight.

"What am I supposed to do here," she said, more to herself. "I don't want to hand you over, but I can't leave you here."

"Why not? I'll be fine," I opined. She shook her head again.

"I'm not going to leave a kid in a hospital surrounded by infected," she said in anger. "You're in a wheelchair, for crying out loud."

"I can get around," I interrupted. She lifted her arms and then dropped them in defeat.

"Come on," she said as she opened the door. "Maybe we'll figure something on the way out."

Angie walked beside me in silence while I pushed the wheels of my chair. I noticed her nervous glances that made me wonder if she was anxious about what to do with me, or whether I would tell someone about her own illness. I had already decided I wouldn't tell, but I hadn't told her. Exposing Angie wouldn't help my situation, and I wouldn't wish it on anyone else.

We weaved past the shuffling bodies without incident. While they all had a similar, crazed look on their faces with those fogged-up eyes, some with bloodied hands and clothes, they had remained mostly human. Others looked as if something had pulled them through a shredder. Blood oozed from their tattered necks and torn flesh. I avoided looking at any of them for too long.

We reached the red door at the end of the hall, and we saw it sat at a crack. There wasn't any sign of Jonesy or Chuck inside the small space that looked like a janitor's closet. They must have moved on. A door connected to the room on the other side, and Angie stepped forward to grab the door handle. She glanced over her shoulder.

"Let's move slowly. I don't have any more weapons, but we should be fine if we take it slowly." She opened the door at a crack to peer out, and then motioned me to follow. We ventured into another hallway. This one wasn't as pristine as the other ones we had come across. It didn't look as if patients or visitors used it—more like an access area for maintenance crews or something. The floor was an unpolished gray, and there weren't any windows. White fluorescent lights guided us to a green door at the end.

I looked up at Angie and knew I had to somehow convince her not to hand me over. My life was short as it was, but I couldn't let it end in a hospital where doctors poked and prodded me for research purposes. I couldn't let that happen, not after my sister had given her life so I could have a notion of a normal one. Alison killed herself so they wouldn't need to poke me anymore. I would need a compelling argument, but I had no idea how to do that. I looked up at Angie, and she diverted her gaze.

"Does Jonesy know about your cancer?" I asked tentatively. When she didn't react I added, "I mean, he must have noticed something."

Her eyes fell on me, but she remained silent, as if she were thinking it over.

"If he knows he hasn't told," she said absently. I sensed she hadn't thought about it that much, but she'd now realized that he must have known. For one, Jonesy had seen her exit the balcony without a problem while moments later Burke had found his end past those frosted-glass doors that apparently sat loaded with crazies. Given their jobs, I wouldn't be surprised if there had been other such incidents.

"He must be a good friend if he didn't give you away." She stopped suddenly and turned to me.

"I know what you're doing, kid, and you can stop."

I peered up at her eyes blinking and giving her my most pathetic facial expression—including my infamous pout.

"All right, you win." She stomped off, and I rushed after her.

"What do you mean?" I asked as if I were clueless.

"I mean, we will find your way out, nick a car, and then think of something else, okay?"

I looked at her in disbelief. "You promise?"

She turned to face me. "I promise." It was probably the fluorescent lighting above us, but it seemed as if the darkness had disappeared from her hazel eyes. The sight produced a wide grin on my face.

"Okay then," I said, "but don't call me kid."

Angie's face twitched, but remained straight. She turned to the door and walked away, shaking her head. I couldn't wipe the grin off my face. There wasn't much of a plan, but she wouldn't turn me in. Nothing else mattered at that point.

Angie went ahead to open the door before returning her gaze with a puzzled look. I bit the inside of my cheek and smirked. It wasn't a surprise to me when widening the opening revealed a set of stairs.

"I thought you used this way to sneak out with your sister," she said, pointing at the stairs.

"Those were the walking years," I said with a shrug. She let out an exaggerated breath.

"All right then. Let's go," she said and bent to pick me up. I wasn't afraid of my weight, and I was short for my age, but Angie, although tough, was on the petite side. We would have made an odd picture, I thought, when a cold rush of air made me shiver, and I remembered my flimsy hospital gown.

"Angie," I said, my voice lined with doubt.

"Yeah?" she said with a groan as she took the first steps down the stairs.

"Does my naked butt stick out?"

"God, I hope not."

7

The steps ended at a steel fire exit. The exit opened into a narrow alley that smelled of decaying garbage, which wasn't a surprise considering the row of dumpsters we had to pass before we cleared it. The sunlight that struck my body was a warm welcome on my cold skin. I glanced over the small grassy area and spotted the two trees that had provided my sister and me some shade the last time I'd been here. Memories flooded my mind.

"Your hair is as white as snow," Alison had said when we'd sat under that tree where she had braided my hair.

"Yeah, after a dog has peed in it," I'd said. She had tugged on my hair, and I'd yelped.

"Don't say that! You have beautiful hair." When I had turned to look at her, a colorful scarf hiding her near-bald head, I'd felt the tears sting my eyes. Even with the dark circles under her eyes and sunken cheeks, she had looked so beautiful. She'd just smiled at me and stroked my hair without a hint of envy.

Angie shifted me in her arms, and I tightened my grip around her neck.

"Now what?" I asked, swallowing the lump in my throat. One of the crazies stumbled around a corner, lumbering around as if he were a lost drunk in disguise. He tripped and fell flat on his face with a bone-chilling moan.

"Now, we try to find a car without disturbing the locals," she replied.

Angie carried me across the grass and onto a brick path. The buildings that made up the hospital loomed at our side. The road parallel to the hospital felt eerily deprived of the sounds of car engines and honking motorists. I could see groups of people milling around beyond another grassy lawn and a low wall, but they were too far off for us to see their eyes. Their behavior, though, suggested crazies.

"What if your people find us?" I asked.

"Then we'll have to come up with a different plan, but I'm hopeful they're still on the other side of the hospital."

"How come?" Angie again shifted me to get a better grip. Her breathing became heavier with every step.

"The plan was to exit with all the cancer patients from the closest access point, which means the underground parking garage on the other side of the building."

Angie moved closer to a fence and kneeled to put me down. Rocks dug into my butt, which I chose to ignore. I didn't feel very comfortable in my flimsy hospital gown out in the open.

"Stay here for a minute," she said and sprinted away from the fence. My mouth hung open in shock as I watched her run across the lawn and hop over the low wall.

"Sure, I'll stay right here," I muttered under my breath. Then I hurled a rock after her and bit out,

"Where else would I go?"

In my mind, I collected a decent amount of curse words I would throw at Angie while my head whipped from side to side to watch for bad things coming. I felt as helpless as a newborn baby, naked butt and all. From my position, I couldn't see much except for the grass ahead and the wall beyond. To my right stood the building we had just come from; a couple of benches with a dried-up fountain obscured my view to the left. I didn't hear anything of the sounds of the city I knew, except for the chilling moans of the crazies. A few of them hovered at the fountain, and another lumbered on the lawn, but they had no interest in me. I rubbed a hand over my head. The sun started to burn my scalp. My stomach twisted and turned—I felt sick. I didn't want to be alone out here.

"Please come back, Angie. Please come back." I didn't even realize I was softly chanting the words. Then I heard the sound of boots. A moment later Angie's head popped up over the wall, and I sighed in relief.

"You okay?" she asked when she sat down next to me. "You look a little pale."

I nodded, not sure if I could trust my voice. Angie's presence boosted my confidence.

"There are a couple of cars on the road we can try. The doors are open," she said pointing in the direction she had come from.

"Can't you hot-wire one?" I said, glad to have found my voice.

"Do I look like a common car thief, kid?"

"I thought they'd teach you that stuff in the army, and don't call me kid," I said and punched her in the shoulder. Unfazed she lifted an eyebrow at that.

"I'm not with the army, kid," she replied, emphasizing the word *kid*, but that's not what my eyes perked up at.

"Then what?" I asked, curious, but as if she realized she had said too much, her cheeks flushed, and she diverted her gaze.

"We have to go," she said and scooped me up from the ground.

We cornered another wall, and Angie stepped onto the road that led to the hospital's main entry. The road circled around the dried-up fountain and then back to the gates that separated the hospital grounds from the street. Motorists used the area for patient drop-offs.

Angie shifted me up in her arms and smirked at me. I smiled. We were almost out and in the clear. Her boot had taken one step off the curb when a loud voice made her freeze.

"Sergeant Meadow, we have been looking for you. Are you all right?" the voice said. A couple of the crazies by the fountain stirred, but two soldiers were quick to react and took them out with bullets to the head. They must have had silencers on their rifles because the sounds of their shots were mere pop, pops to the powerful sound of the automatics I had gotten used to. "Sergeant," the voice repeated, "are you all right?"

My heart hammered in my chest while I watched Angie frozen in place. I gripped the back of her neck and squeezed it tight. My eyes locked on hers, trying to get a reaction, but Angie just stood there, unmoving, my limp body in her hands, my naked butt still sticking out. Oh God, soldiers were about to surround me, ready to send me off to God knows where while my butt stuck out.

Angie came back to life, and for the briefest moments, she glanced at me. Her eyes were wide and glassy, which made them almost sparkle in the bright sunlight. Then they closed, and she made a half turn to the men approaching us from the hospital.

"No," I tried to say, but it came out more like a whimper. "But you promised." My voice was firmer with that.

"What's this?" one of two soldiers who now stood in front of us said.

"Captain Decker, sir," Angie said. "This is one of the patients who tried to evade us, sir." Her voice was stone cold. She was a robot—she had to be. How could she promise me and now hand me over like that?

"And she has to be carried," Decker said.

"She's paralyzed, sir. Took off in her wheelchair, but we had to ditch it." The man frowned at me for a moment and then shook his head.

"Never mind, any word from Private Jones?" he asked. For the first time in a while, Angie moved her head.

"He isn't back yet?"

"No," the other man said. I recognized the tall, dark lieutenant from when he'd stepped out of the elevator before everything had turned to shit. That bright smile had turned into a frown, but his jade eyes still stood out, and looked worried.

I zoned out from the conversation. I was glad the soldiers hadn't found Chuck, but it could also mean he was dead already, eaten by one of the crazies. I couldn't help Chuck. I couldn't even help myself. Tears welled up in my eyes. I didn't want to cry, and I bit the inside of my cheek until the coppery taste of blood filled my mouth. Anything to distract me from all this—this conversation, these men, and the darkness that had reclaimed Angie's eyes.

Someone tried to take me out of Angie's arms, and as much as I wanted to get away from her darkened gaze, I wanted her to see me. I wanted her to see what would happen to me. My hand tightened on her collar, and I gripped her vest.

"You promised," I said when I felt hands tug at my waist. "You promised."

Angie didn't move; she just watched, her body as limp as my legs.

"You promised," I shouted over the soldier's shoulder as he dragged me off and she watched. Before the soldier carrying me went down a set of steps, I caught one more glance of Angie. That tall lieutenant I had seen before stood by her side, a hand on her shoulder, but she ignored him, her eyes still on me. It was what I wanted, but I guess I hadn't expected to see the amount of pain on her face as I did.

8

I woke with at start. A hazy blur masked my vision, and for a second I worried the infection had clouded my eyes with that funky mist, making me one of the crazies. It turned out the tantrum I had thrown coming down the steps had given them a reason to sedate me. My body lay strapped to a gurney within the darkened bowels of the hospital's underground parking garage. Those idiots had even strapped my legs. It took me a minute to get a grip on my surroundings. My vision was blurred, my eyelids heavy, and my head even heavier.

The gurney I lay on stood in a cleared section of the parking garage. Five medium-sized buses stood in line at the entry. Gaunt-looking faces with worried expressions stared out the windows of the buses. Among them, I recognized the old gossip lady named Maggie. She seemed in a vivid, almost hysterical discussion with a young man in a uniform. I guessed they had informed her about her husband turning into one of the crazies. The soldier's helmet bobbed on his head while he nodded and held his hands up in a defensive manner as if to calm the old woman down.

To make room for the buses, cars had been maneuvered to the exit side of the lot. Heavy-duty spotlights stood along the exit ramp that led out of the underground parking garage—guarded by soldiers to prevent unwanted guests from entering. Night had fallen on the city. I must have been out for a couple of hours. Several patients, all stuck in beds, stood in my little corner. Most of them looked too sick to travel by bus. To my right I could see the door to the hospital and the elevators that would lead up to the main entry.

The door to the hospital swung open, and Captain Decker strolled out, followed by his minions, including the tall, dark lieutenant and Sergeant Meadow. I balled my fists and tugged at my restraints until they bit into my wrists, ready to shout the first curse words that popped into my head. I wouldn't let them take me without a fight, even if it would only be a verbal one. My mouth opened, but then I closed it shut. There was something off-putting in their demeanor.

Captain Decker waved his arms and shouted at one of his soldiers. "Get your men out there and hold them off. We need time to get the buses out of here."

The soldier turned on his heels, shouted to gather some men, and then paced up the ramp.

"This is getting out of hand too fast. The first two floors are overrun. The evacuation crews will never be able to get to the rest of the patients," the tall, dark lieutenant said. "And getting them out by helicopters will take too long."

"That is not our problem, Lieutenant," Captain Decker said. "It is our job to get these buses to the airport safely, and that's what we'll do. As soon as our access route clears, we move out—get them ready."

With a nod, the lieutenant jogged off in the direction of the buses.

"Any word on Jones?" Decker asked. Angie shook her head.

"None, sir." Her head eased to the area where I lay on my stretcher. Our eyes met, but Angie's dark gaze seemed to pass straight through me. "What about them?"

Decker followed her gaze.

"See if you can fit as many of them on the buses. We can't wait for new ones to arrive. Use the aisles," he said. "The rest …"

He fell silent after that. Angie's face hardened. She nodded and started to make her way to us. I glanced at the faces that surrounded me in the other beds. Jarrod and Gary were among them. Jarrod gazed at the ceiling as if it were the most interesting thing he had ever seen. His eyes were glassy, and he didn't even seem to blink. I guessed Gary to be the luckiest of all of us—he had already checked out, at least, his brain had.

Angie drew closer, and I ground my teeth. I wanted to rationalize what she had done, or more to the point—hadn't done—but I couldn't subside the anger.

"Come to gloat?" I said in a venomous tone. She gave me a hard look but didn't answer. Instead, she pushed my gurney to the back of the pack into a dark corner. She glanced over her shoulder and then at me.

"Just shut up and play dead," she said in a hushed

tone. My eyes widened when she undid my straps. I wanted to hug her at that point but did as she had said and lay unmoving. Without another word, she moved to the front and gestured to a group of men. The soldiers came running. After Angie waved her hand in the air and barked some orders, they started carting the beds to the buses. One bed after another, soldiers transported my fellow patients from our little corner, but the process was slow. As the captain had mentioned, there wasn't enough room.

There were about five of us left, including Jarrod and Gary, when a scream echoed from the parking garage's walls. A chill ran through my bones. A man's voice filled with an indescribable agony filled the open space. Then there was silence. It lasted for mere seconds before gunshots replaced it. They sounded louder than anything I'd heard before. The booms bounced off the parking garage's wall and repeated themselves over and over again. Soldiers, sounding their battle cries, firing their weapons, tried to hold the ramp, but the mass of lumbering bodies forced them back.

I clamped my hands over my head in a vain attempt to protect my ears. My head whipped around in search of some way to get myself out of this, but what was I supposed to do? The hospital entry and the elevators looked to be, what, about fifty paces away from me. It could just as well be the other side of the world. I would never reach them crawling around on my arms. My fist slammed into my upper leg. *Stupid, stupid,* echoed in my head.

The engines of buses revved and the smell of diesel wafted around me. Soldiers dispersed at the foot of the ramp. A Hummer parked next to one of the buses took off, building speed before it hit the ramp. Crazies slammed into the front grill and bounced to the sides. Combined with the heavy machine gun mounted on the roof, shooting at anything in its path, the Hummer plowed a way forward. The buses followed in their wake. Soldiers from all sides came running for the vehicles. Shots fired and crazies fell, but the soldiers were not without casualties. Men caught by the hungry teeth-snapping creatures fell to the ground where a wall of bodies swallowed them up. Screaming, they disappeared in the midst of horror. The ones able to cling to the buses forced their bodies inside, cramping in one after another until nothing else would fit.

A soldier grabbed the frame of an open window. One of the crazies clung to his leg, but the soldier managed to hang on. He screamed as the crazy's teeth sunk into his calf. His pants ripped along with the skin and tendons underneath. Within moments, the soldier's arms started to tremble, and his head twitched to a side. His jaw stretched open, further than I had ever seen. Growling, he scrambled through the window. Screams erupted from inside while the bus drove on.

My heart slammed inside my chest, hoping, praying Angie's words had been truthful when she said the crazies had no taste for cancer patients. Then another thing she had said rocked my mind. She had said they might attack if agitated. I looked up at the bodies pouring down the ramp. They seemed to qualify as agitated.

Desperate, I searched around me for something. The vehicles were gone, although there were still soldiers firing their weapons. Pipes leading up the wall caught my attention. Maybe I could climb one of them. The thought alone nearly shut my body down, but I had to try something. Unable to reach the pipe, I used Gary's bed to push myself off to get some momentum going. All it did was set Gary rolling towards the crazies. I looked down and saw the brakes to my gurney locked on the tiny wheels. Angie had put on the brakes. Violently cursing, I hung over the edge of the gurney.

"You about done, kid?" a voice said. My head snapped up. Combined with the lessening, but still loud gunshots, I hadn't noticed Angie by my side.

Out of a strange combination of desperation, fear, and relief, I shouted at her, "Don't call me a goddamned kid!"

The gunfire drew closer around us. Without a comment on my little outburst, Angie turned to the men. Five of them came running as if trying to escape hell. The crazies behind them surely made it look as if creatures that clawed themselves out of the debts of hell were chasing them. Mid-run they would swirl, draw their weapons, and fire uncontrolled rounds at the oncoming onslaught. They hit everything, torsos, legs, shattered windshields of parked cars, but none of them seemed to remember to add a headshot. Angie and Jonesy had remembered when we first came across the crazies. These men acted like Burke, and it would get them killed.

"Get your shit together," Angie shouted. "Aim for the heads."

The men either didn't hear or were too scared for it to register. Angie grabbed my arm and swung me over her shoulder like a wounded soldier. I managed not to hit my head on the butt of the rifle that hung across her back. She must have acquired a new one. Avoiding the rifle, I grabbed a handful of her armored vest to hold myself steady.

Boots were pounding, and I watched the stretcher disappear into the shadows. I could still see Jarrod lying there on his gurney. He seemed frozen like Gary, but I knew his reasons. Maybe they had given Jarrod something to keep quiet like me. I hoped so.

Between the shouts and rapid automatic gunfire, I heard a crash. Hanging over Angie's shoulder, it wasn't easy to differentiate anything except for the rifle on her back and her butt. That made me visualize my own butt sticking out, and I shoved the thought aside. I lifted my head and saw Gary face down on the asphalt. Crazies awkwardly stumbled and fell as they tried to hurdle the toppled gurney. Unsteady legs trampled Gary's body as if he were a rug. I looked away and focused on Angie's ragged breathing and spitting commands.

"Get inside," she shouted. I thought she meant the hospital, but we passed the door with the milling crazies behind it and headed for a small shed-like building. Bodies and boots closed in on me, but I kept my head down and couldn't see who was who or what was what. Shouts and gunshots hammered my ears until I was sure they would leave permanent damage. A door slammed closed, and the gunshots stopped.

Heavy breathing filled the tiny room. Besides two soldiers, Angie, and me, the room had a desk with a computer. In the corner sat a small table with a coffee maker on top and an extra chair. A rack with keys hung on the only wall without windows. I didn't wish to inspect the other sides of the small guard post because I knew the windows would show the rage-filled faces of the crazies with their funky white eyes.

Angie had shrugged me off her shoulder and forced me to crawl under the desk. With trembling hands, she pulled at my hospital gown to smooth it over my legs. It was the first time I'd seen anything that resembled fear in her. That scared me. The hard lines on her face felt more reassuring, although her jaw clenched.

"Why did you bring the science project?" one of the soldiers said. Angie's hands balled into fists and whipped her head around to face him. I couldn't see her expression, but the man reacted by dropping his eyes to the ground and lowered the helmet on his head. As if something had swept over her to change her resolve, Angie's shoulders straightened, and she readied her weapon.

The other soldier kept attempting to load his gun, but his shaking hands kept him from sliding the clip in. Unnerved by this, Angie got to her knees, grabbed the clip, and slammed it in. Just about then, fists started to pound on the windows.

I forced myself to look but wished I hadn't. Pale faces with mouths strung open wide and funky white eyes pounded the glass with bloodied fists. The plain wooden door shook from the pressure of the weight of bodies outside the room. A firm hand pressed my head down.

"Just stay down and keep calm. They won't go for you if you don't agitate them, remember," Angie said in a whisper, her voice calm and reassuring. Glancing sideways, I could tell her expression was tense.

"Shit, shit, shit!" one of the men started to chant. I didn't look up to see who it was, but I figured it to be the one having the trouble loading the rifle. The thumps on the glass increased. A loud crack froze the movement of air inside the small room. We all held our breaths, and I imagined a few prayers were said for the benefit of the glass. Unfortunately—without effect.

A fist plowed through the window, leaving the hand cut and bloodied. Bodies pressed against the glass until it shattered. Angie and the two soldiers opened fire. I clamped my hands over my ears. More glass shattered, and one of the crazies dove nose first into the room. Angie stomped a foot on its back and then aimed her gun at its head and fired. One of the soldiers screamed as clawing fingers grabbed his uniform and pulled him into their midst. His handgun clattered to the ground near my feet. The man screamed and screamed while the other soldier fired his weapon in a desperate attempt to free his friend. Angie pushed him to a side and fired her gun. The screaming stopped.

Angie pulled a tight circle of a constant spray of bullets. One of the crazies made a grab for the remaining soldier and pulled him close. A man the size of a football player, with arms as large as an average person's legs, jerked the soldier off balance. The man's enormous jaws opened and stretched. I reached for the gun on the floor by my feet. It was my intention to shoot the football player, but he already had his teeth sunken deep into the soldier's neck. The soldier's body twitched without much of a struggle. Blood gushed down his neck. His eyes flung from side to side, pleading for someone to save him. The short bursts of Angie's automatic rifle hammered in my ears while I watched the color fade from the soldier's eyes.

When the eyes had drowned inside that funky white fog, the football player released the soldier as if he had lost his appetite. The body twitched, and the irises swimming behind the fog seemed to focus on me. I swallowed hard at the sight. My hand trembled, and I added my other hand to steady the gun. The soldier stretched his jaw as if he was using it for the first time, and then snapped it shut. His nose went up into the air, and a bloodied hand reached out to grab me. I didn't wait to see whether he liked what he smelled. I pulled the trigger.

The shooting in the room stopped. Angie turned to face me. Her eyes fell on the gun before they trailed the barrel to the soldier and then came back to me. I jumped at the discharge of her weapon. Angie had shot another crazy too close for comfort before she dropped to her knees. My gaze had returned to the soldier with a hole in his left cheek. Unlike the blood gushing from his neck, this looked like a black, oil-like substance that seemed too thick to be blood.

Without consideration, Angie pulled the gun from my hand while shoving me back underneath the desk. She pressed in after me with the dead soldier's body in tow. She used the body to hide us, but even underneath a desk, we should have been visible.

Several crazies plowed over the windowsill into the room. They struggled to stand on top of the pile of arms and legs of the fallen. Moans that seemed to emerge from dark caves sent shivers down my spine.

I glanced at my trembling hands as images of the dead soldier hauntingly flashed across my mind. Unable to make them stop, I clasped my hands together on my lap. Angie's hand slipped over them. Her eyes told me she had her own problems keeping her head cool. Her breaths came in quick bursts as did mine, and I figured her heart was pounding as fast as mine.

Neither of us dared to move with the crazies milling around while they moaned and sniffed the room. When they finally settled down, Angie spoke in a low whisper. "You okay?"

My heart was caught in my throat. I sensed I might not be able to control the volume of my voice and nodded instead. Angie shifted her position, a painful grimace on her face. The way she sat angled underneath the desk must have tortured her back.

"Listen," she said and then hesitated. "What happened back there ... I didn't want ..." She broke off.

"It's okay," I said when I found my voice. "I understand you didn't have much of a choice."

"No, that's not it—I'm not part of this," she said a little too loudly. One of the crazies stirred, and we both held our breath. Frustration was evident on Angie's face. When the air settled, she resumed.

"This thing is a lot bigger than you know, and I wish I could explain, but there are things ..." She let out a huff of frustration. "I'm not the kind of person to ship people off to their death for the sake of science."

I watched as her intense eyes bore into me. "I'm actually with the FBI," she said. "My partner and I, we're searching for evidence to prosecute the ones responsible for releasing this virus."

"I know," I said. Angie looked at me with an astonished expression that made me smile, releasing some of the tension in my arms.

"You knew I was with the FBI?" she asked.

"No, but you saved me—I'm here, right?" I said and narrowed my eyes at her. "Who's your partner? That tall dude with the bright eyes?"

Angie nodded while she spoke. "Yeah, his name is Mars."

"Like the candy?" I asked, confused.

Angie slumped while a breath of air rolled over

her lips.

"You're something else, you know." She looked around for a minute as if she needed to check if the crazies were still in the room.

"I have an older sister," she said. "She and my mom live on the West Coast."

"Don't tell me," I said. "I remind you of her."

"Nah, you remind me of me," she said with a smirk. "I think I know now what she had to endure."

9

After a while of sitting in one of the most awkward positions I had ever found myself in, Angie decided to peek around. The remaining crazies in the small guard post had resumed their foot-to-foot shuffle and had averted their attention. Within the same moment, Angie had poked her head out from under the desk, she retreated back in. Her wide eyes and pale face were self-explanatory. It didn't prevent her from voicing her discomfort.

"This is one major cluster-fu…" She swallowed the rest when she caught my glare. I couldn't contain a grin.

"Aren't we supposed to walk straight by them?" I asked. If the crazies didn't have an interest in us—and they seemed calm for the moment—then we should be able to pass them.

"Don't you mean I'll do the walking and carry you," Angie replied. I gave her a dirty look, but she spoke again before I could retort.

"They seem to be stuck in the windows." At the frowned look I gave her, she gestured out the desk.

With some pulling and tugging on my legs, I managed to pull myself up and out to peek around the room. Angie was right. The crazies had gotten themselves stuck in the window frames. Now they were just hanging there, squashed like three or four hot dogs in one bun. The crazies would hang there until Christmas as long as nothing drew their attention.

"I'm not going to crawl over them," I said as I lowered myself down.

Angie shrugged. "We'll have to think of something." With a grunt, she shoved away what remained of the soldier's body we had hidden behind and slipped out from underneath the desk. She stayed low to the ground. One of the crazies must have caught her movement because it shifted with a moan. The others reacted in the manner of synchronized swimmers. Their nostrils flared for a moment, but then they settled down into their idle positions.

Simultaneously our gazes shifted to the door where we could hear a soft thumping. Inside the tiny space, dead bodies covered the floor, and almost-dead bodies balanced on the windowsills. The crazies had us surrounded. I eyed up at Angie.

"Now what?" I asked. She lifted her shoulder in a shrug and opened her mouth to speak when a shot rang out. We both cringed reflexively, but it was the body of one of the crazies that went down with a thump. Thick, black blood oozed from his cracked skull. Bam! Another one went down.

"Here, zombie, zombie, zombie. Here, zombie," someone called out.

Angie and I both looked at each other in shock and spoke his name in unison: "Chuck!" The biggest smile flew across her face. It occurred to me that he called the crazies zombies, which didn't seem like a bad thing to call them. Why hadn't I thought of that?

Another shot and another body went down. Enticed by the sound, or if their flailing nostrils were any sign, more by the smell of something good, the crazies or zombies started to stir. Chuck repeated his call while one by one the zombies entangled their limbs from one another.

My smile grew, but Angie's face turned dark.

"What is it?" I asked. Frustrated, she grabbed a rifle from the ground and started to check the dead soldier for ammunition. Angie had to wait for the rapid gunfire to die down before she could answer my question so I could hear.

"What does that idiot think he's doing?" she said through gritted teeth. I watched the zombies struggle and wriggle themselves out of their idiotic positions with a ferociousness that a brick wall wouldn't be able to stop. It made me realize what Angie feared. It wasn't Chuck she worried about—he would eventually be able to just walk out of here—but Jonesy wouldn't be able to flee from them, and the shooting would attract the zombies to his position. Two more shots rang out followed by a ding and the soft sound of sliding doors. Angie grinned.

"Maybe he isn't that stupid."

Jonesy had fled using the elevator. Not wasting our opportunity, she extended a hand to help me out from under the desk. She picked me off the floor, and with a grunt, she sat me down on the desk. My eyes darted across the small room to take in the carnage. Bodies of all sizes surrounded the small building. Most were ripped to shreds by a barrage of bullets; some still moved.

Angie checked the door. Widening the opening showed none of the, I guessed, zombies that had besieged the guard post.

Back inside she scooped me from the desk. I felt grateful that she hadn't decided on the over-the-shoulder position. When we stepped around the building, my mouth dropped open.

As if he were Moses himself, a wall of shuffling bodies parted for the old man with an oxygen chart—and a walker.

"Chuck!" I called out, delighted to see him. His chest heaved, but he made his way to us with strong strides.

"Jeez, I thought you'd bought it before you showed up here," Angie huffed out. Chuck looked up with a crooked smile, and I felt relieved to see his wrinkled face.

"We thought the same of you," he said.

"Nice ride," I said, pointing at the walker that held his oxygen cart in a basket. Chuck smirked.

"How did you know we were here?" Angie asked. He chuckled at that. A mischievous smile clung to his face.

"That friend of yours won't be too happy with you," he said and then broke out in a coughing fit.

When he caught his breath, he told us how when we hadn't exited the building, he had forced Jonesy back inside at gunpoint.

"We gained access to a security room when your buddies evacuated. That thing had more screens than an electronics store," he said, exasperated. "We saw everything that happened and thought you might need a hand."

"That we did," Angie said.

Chuck explained that he had acted as a decoy for Jonesy and simultaneously had urged the zombies to follow him. Once Chuck had succeeded in drawing them away from the guard post, Jonesy had no trouble taking them out. After clearing a path, Jonesy had fled to the security room on the second floor using the elevator. From there he could follow our progress. Now all we had to do was wait for the zombies to calm down and ride the elevator up to the second floor. We could have taken the stairs, but Chuck wasn't up for it.

Jonesy faced us, arms crossed, jaws tight when the elevator doors slid open on the second floor. Bodies drilled with holes covered the hallway floor. At least six had found their end near the elevator with several more lying dead further down the hall. All the while, Jonesy just stood there leaning casually against the wall with his sunglasses still perched on his nose. This could mean anything, but I feared the worst. Still, I felt relieved to see him. Besides, he didn't aim his glare at me.

"Not now, Jonesy," Angie said when she stepped out carrying me.

"You gave that old goat a gun," Jonesy said, unamused.

"Hey," Chuck said, "I haven't shot you yet, but

that doesn't mean I won't."

Jonesy growled something incomprehensible under his breath.

Angie sat me down on one of those plastic seating arrangements that could be found in the halls on every floor of this building and then turned to Jonesy. "Give me an update," she said.

Jonesy explained what had happened in about a third of the amount of words Chuck had used. When he finished, he added, "You were trying to get her out."

Angie's face flushed red. She took him by the elbow to guide him away from us.

"I saw what you were trying to do on the security monitors—don't deny it," he said before they stepped out of earshot.

Chuck came to sit next to me and rubbed a hand over the fuzzy hair on my head. It felt ice-cold, as if the blood had run and fled from his hand. His face looked a pale white with a bluish sheen on his lips. When I glanced at his oxygen cart, he said in a resigned voice, "There is not much left. But don't you worry, half pint."

"We can find some more," I said and felt the tremor in my voice.

He smiled but didn't answer. Instead, he padded my head and said, "That is a pretty neat trick we've got going, avoiding the zombies and shit."

I swallowed at the tightness in my throat and produced a smile that I hoped didn't resemble a grimace. "Yeah, pretty neat."

I glanced over to the two soldiers arguing. Well, it wasn't much of an argument—Angie did most of the talking. When they finished, Jonesy disappeared into a connecting hall.

Angie sank down the wall across from us, rifle perched on her lap. She looked exhausted. Strains of hair sprang loosely from her Mohawk braid and all kinds of gunk stuck to her face and clothes. I figured my flimsy white gown would probably look worse, so I didn't check. Angie dropped the back of her head against the wall, and it seemed to take some effort to pull it back up. I didn't appreciate the expression on her face when our eyes finally met. She looked concerned.

"He called in the cavalry," she said in a low voice.

"Son of a bitch," Chuck bit out. "You can't trust anyone these days."

My body felt tired. I didn't know what time it was, but we had cruised around this hospital since the break of dawn without breakfast. So the gears in my head seemed to spin a little slower, but when it hit, it hit me hard.

"They're coming back for us," I said. The fear in my own voice caught me off guard. Chuck and Angie both looked at me as if I were something fragile, ready to break. They were right, but it wasn't what I wanted to be. My hands clamped down on the edge of the plastic chairs until the rims bit into my fingers. I wanted to be strong, but couldn't ignore the tears stinging my eyes.

In one swift movement, Angie crossed the floor to

kneel in front of me. She placed a comforting hand on my cheek while the hand of an old man whom I had met the night before proved a solid comfort on my back. It seemed surreal, but I listened to Angie's words and held on to them.

"Just remembered what I promised, okay? I'll find a way." Before I could reply, Jonesy stepped around the corner, pushing an old fifties-model wheelchair. The thing seemed to come straight out of a mad scientist movie. He stopped to eye the three of us. Angie backed off with a sigh. As he stepped in closer, he reached out to help me onto the chair.

"I can do it," I said in a sharp tone. His hands shot up in defense, and he stepped back.

A loud rumble seemed to come from outside. Jonesy's head snapped up along with the rest of us. Our heads tilted as if we could see the spinning of the blades cutting through the darkening sky. We couldn't see anything, nothing but the white ceiling with its fluorescent lights in contrast to the blood-smeared walls. I couldn't see it, but I knew it was there. The helicopter coming to get us had arrived.

10

When the sound of the rotors subsided after they must have landed on the roof and shut down the engine, I glanced at the people around me. Chuck sat across from me in one of the plastic chairs. He stared at the ceiling with a grim expression. Darkness hovered in Angie's eyes, fixed on Jonesy. Not impressed, Jonesy held Angie's gaze with a grin plastered on his face.

"That's our ride," he said gleefully.

"I'm not coming with you," I said. I wish I sounded more convincing, but my voice came out a broken mess. I didn't want to go through that again. I didn't want to be strapped to a bed. The sound of something clattering to the ground drew my attention, and I shifted my gaze to a staircase door a little further down from us.

"You don't have a choice," Jonesy said. "You want to stay here among those mindless corpses? So what if they don't want to eat you? You'll never make it on your own."

I ignored Jonesy's remark and noticed Chuck's focus on the same direction. He must have heard it too. My gaze shifted between the shuffling sounds coming from beyond that open door and the standoff between the two soldiers. For once, I was glad for the stupid sunglasses Jonesy wore on his face. They protected me from a glare that I was sure would cut straight through me. Jonesy shifted his attention to Angie, who hadn't moved.

"And don't think you'll be able to help them. They know we're here," he said while he nodded at Chuck and me. With one hand, he removed the sunglasses without taking his gaze from Angie. "And don't think I don't know what you are. You are just as much one of them." Jonesy pointed an accusing finger at Chuck and me.

Except Chuck's attention wasn't on Jonesy. His focus was on the fingers that curled around the doorpost. "Did you really think I wouldn't notice?" Jonesy added. Angie took in a sharp breath that came out in a calming breeze. I wondered if she had seen what Chuck and I saw or if she had heard the scuffle.

"No," she said, her voice calm. "I didn't think you'd hold it over me after the shit we've been through."

"It's nothing personal. You know that," he said, putting the sunglasses back on his nose. "But like the briefing said, the sacrifice of the few is necessary to ensure the survival of the many."

With that, Jonesy raised his rifle and pointed it at Angie's chest. She returned the gesture by raising her own rifle. Through what seemed like a blur of movement, my heart stopped at the sight of the two soldiers, face to face, guns raised. My heart slammed back into motion, hammering against my chest.

Slow and calculated, Chuck gripped the handlebars of his walker to raise himself to a stand. With ease, he backed away from Jonesy, stepping closer to the staircase door.

"Stop moving, old fool," Jonesy said without moving a muscle.

At the door, the hand morphed into a complete figure in jeans and a red T-shirt. A black, oily substance oozed from several holes in its torso. Torn flesh hung where there used to be an arm. There seemed to be a confusion going on behind the white fog that swam across its eyes. Caught in the white goo, its irises shifted from left to right. As Chuck shifted between the door and Jonesy, the zombie's nose shot up and sniffed the air.

"What the hell are you doing, old man," Jonesy said.

"A foolish attempt to save your miserable life," Chuck answered. Jonesy's head twitched, but he refused to pull his gaze away from Angie. She still hadn't moved an inch and didn't seem to have any intention to do so. Angie could see perfectly well what was happening behind Jonesy's back.

"Get your ass back here, you old bastard." Jonesy seemed to be losing his patience.

Another figure appeared in the doorway. This one wore a once-white doctor's coat, now covered in blood oozing from his scalp down his face and neck.

The two zombies acted calmly—confused but calm, as if they couldn't sense the reason that had brought them to this floor. Then I realized the reason had to be Chuck. Those funky eyes didn't help the zombies a thing in their hunt to relieve their hunger. It had to be their sense of smell that must have brought them here. Jonesy had been the one to attract them, but Chuck seemed to be the one to confuse them.

Our bodies, under siege by the accelerated growth of cells, must give off an odor that repelled them, and now Chuck was standing between them and their candy. Chuck actually was attempting to save Jonesy's life.

"Just stay calm," Chuck said.

"There are infected in the staircase," Angie said in her low, calm voice.

"Bullshit," Jonesy exclaimed, refusing to take his eyes of Angie. "Infected can't climb stairs." The words had barely left his mouth when the zombie in the red shirt stretched open its jaw. A wad of black gunk slithered from its torn lips. It hissed and stepped into the hall.

Jonesy flinched at the sound. Immediately, Angie's eyes grew wider. Would Jonesy shoot her? My hands gripped the wheels of my old chair. I didn't know what I'd do, but I knew I had to be ready to move. Jonesy eased his head aside to glance over his shoulder.

"Easy," Angie whispered. His feud with Angie momentarily forgotten, Jonesy slightly turned to get a better look. Chuck released his walker to spread his arms wide. He was trying to spread his scent to mask Jonesy. Having caught up with the old man's thinking, I spun the wheels of my chair to move to his side.

"Ash," Angie said, drawing out my name. "What

are you doing?" I eyed her over my shoulder. She remained in her fighting stance, rifle raised, but the barrel had shifted slightly and aimed at the zombies now instead of Jonesy.

"They don't like how we smell," I said in a hushed voice. "If we keep our scent between Jonesy and them, they won't attack. Maybe we can lock ourselves inside a room or something." The words formed as if I hadn't thought them through. Was I ready to protect Jonesy when all he wanted was to turn us in—including Angie? I didn't want to die, but I didn't want anybody else's death to be my fault either. In the end, would it matter how we died? It wasn't as if death weren't coming for me soon enough.

Chuck glanced down with a pleased expression. Did that mean he was proud of me? There was no time to figure out what that look meant. I raised my arms into the air. The decrepit bodies hovered in front of us. The tension swelling in my chest eased. Fear of these creatures relented, and I realized they couldn't help what they had become. A virus had done this to them. The scientist waiting to set their needles into my flesh stirred a greater fear than these zombies did.

The zombie that wore the doctor's coat twitched. His head snapped to the side, and a deep-rooted moan clawed its way up its throat. The sound sent chills through my bones. Moans echoed up from down the staircase. Slow, heavy footsteps climbed the steps. Others followed. I swallowed hard and resisted the urge to retreat.

Feet shifted behind me, and I glanced over my shoulder. Angie had stepped in closer and stood almost at Jonesy's side. As the probable choice on the menu, Jonesy seemed hesitant to move, as if motion might trigger the zombies. He had lowered his weapon, so it wasn't pointing at Angie anymore. With his back still partially turned to me, he looked over his shoulder.

A body slammed into the open door. A bulk of a man over six feet tall and six feet wide clawed at the door with chubby fingers to keep him steady. Blood and that oily stuff smeared his face and stained his shirt. A snarl showed blackened teeth. The giant tripped, shifting his weight to take a step, and came stumbling into the hall.

I had no choice but to reverse, afraid the bulk of his body would flatten me. Chuck had the same sense to move, and he discarded his walker. Chubby fingers clawed the air, growls filled the room as the oversized zombie landed on the walker, and he almost crushed the thing underneath him. Red shirt's nose flared up, sniffing the air. At its growl, other zombies joined them from out of the stairwell. Shots fired.

I snapped my head around and saw Jonesy firing a barrage of bullets. Bam, bam, bam echoed down the hall while white sparks sprang from his rifle. Jonesy seemed frantic as he reloaded his weapon and fired again. The red shirt's head cracked open. The doctor's chest became a black mist. Fat zombie had managed to get on hands and knees but collapsed when his head went missing.

Angie rushed to my side and started to yank at my chair. My head spun to find Chuck, but a flow of bodies pressed themselves through the opening. For every zombie Jonesy killed, two others passed the door. It wasn't enough. I glanced around, but I didn't see Chuck.

"Ash, let's go!" Angie shouted. I wasn't ready to go, not without Chuck.

"Where's Chuck?" I asked. Before Angie could answer, I saw him—or at least that ugly bathrobe of his. "Chuck," I called out again. His body was half-buried underneath a flock of zombies.

"Ash," Angie shouted. She had been pulling at the chair without success. I released the brake, and Angie reversed my chair.

Jonesy's rifle clicked empty. He cursed as he grabbed his handgun. Six shots later, it clicked empty as well.

Angie had pushed my chair along the hall towards the control room. It didn't take long for Jonesy to speed past us. We were no match for him. He slammed the door closed before we reached it.

"Son of a bitch," Angie called out. I topped it off with an exotic range of curse words of my own.

Angie jerked the chair to a stop. The chair turned until I faced her. More than a dozen zombies had followed us, and though in their standard shuffle mode wouldn't form a threat to us, they seemed to have gone beyond their comfort zone. They looked agitated as hell.

At first glance, I couldn't see a room to hide in.

Patients didn't reside in this section of the hospital. It didn't prevent Angie from finding a spot. She lifted me out of the chair to ease me down to the floor. A row of those plastic chairs bolted to the wall hung next to us. Angie ushered me under it, and then she followed and held the chair in place like a shield. My head slammed into the back wall when Angie's body crammed in. There wasn't a lot of room in the narrow space.

Angie fought to keep the chair upright as legs clambered past it. I couldn't see the reason, but I let her. It wasn't as if I could stop her from doing it anyway.

My eyes locked on that ugly brown bathrobe. I was sure it would have gotten nastier by now. The thought of it prickled tears in my eyes. I had known the old man for no more than a day, and I already liked him better than I liked my dad. Even so, I fought the tears. Chuck wouldn't want me to cry. *Not over my sorry ass*, I could hear his voice say in my head. At least, he wouldn't have to worry about going to the lab.

When the procession of shuffling legs ended, Angie released the chair and plopped down on her back. She exhaled a long breath before she spoke. "You okay, Ash?"

I didn't feel like answering. Everything in my body screamed of an emptiness along with exhaustion. If my mind and heart weren't racing at a million miles a second, I could have fallen asleep underneath those plastic chairs. But the position we lay in didn't allow Angie to see my nod, so I answered, "Fine."

"Yeah, me too," she murmured.

Fists pounded and fingers clawed at the control room door behind us. It wasn't long until we heard glass crack. Angry shouts from Jonesy followed, along with a war cry and screams. Finally, it was only the shuffling of zombie feet until they stopped too. The zombies didn't leave, but they zoned out into their idle state until the next item of interest would stroll by.

I had no sense of time, so I didn't know how long we hid underneath those plastic chairs. However, as soon as the zombies retreated into their idle mode, Angie sprang into action. She hadn't forgotten about the helicopter that had descended onto the hospital's roof. Angie had to remind me when she sat me down in my chair.

She pushed me past the corpses. This was a good thing too because I don't think my arms would have been able to move the chair on my own because they felt too weak. As we passed the ugly robe, I refused to look at it. I wanted to remember Chuck as the wrinkled, old cigarette-smoking man with the Jack Nicholson grin and not how his body had ended up. So I kept my eyes locked on my hands folded in my lap.

"Bye, Chuck," I said in a whisper. Angie must have heard because she squeezed my shoulder.

At a decent pace, but with enough diligence not to

disturb any of the roaming zombies, we took one of the elevators to the third floor. As we stepped into the hallway, it felt eerily quiet. It was as if the entire floor had been deserted, except for a few stray zombies shuffling the halls. Most of the doors to the patients' rooms were closed. On closer inspection, it looked like a couple of doors had been barricaded. We could see piles of tables and chairs through the window in one of the doors. The staff must have tried to isolate themselves along with the patients.

Angie froze when we heard the muffled sounds of gunshots. It sounded as if the noise came from the floor above us.

"They're here," Angie said. I couldn't speak. I didn't know what Angie's plan was, and I felt scared. She picked up the pace, weaving my chair past the zombies, who raised their noses at us as they noticed our approach but seemed to shudder in disgust once they had sniffed us.

The sound of a commotion pulled my gaze to a room of which the door stood open. I could see a man with an arm and leg strapped in some contraption. It seemed we had landed on the orthopedics ward. From the way the man thrashed against his restraints, I figured he must have been infected. I could still hear his moans long after we had passed his room.

More shots fired, and Angie pulled me to a stop in front of a door that stood at a crack. She widened the opening and peered inside as we heard a loud crack.

Not waiting for what it was, she shoved me inside past the bed and into the bathroom. She left me in there, and for a second, I was afraid she wouldn't return. When she did, she threw a bunch of blankets into the tub and then pulled down the shower curtain and placed it on top. Without an explanation, she scooped me out of the chair and placed me in the tub. Too tired to moan about it, I let her while I silently watched how she pulled a packet from her vest and dropped it into the bathtub. As she kneeled beside me, she sucked in a breath as if she needed to compose herself.

"I'm sorry," she said and gave me that hurt look that I had seen before.

"For what?" Before she could answer, a metallic voice boomed down the hall.

"Sergeant Meadow, Private Jones, if you can hear this please respond or try to make a distinct sound if you can't."

Our heads shot to the door. That voice sounded so close. Angie drew in a sharp breath before she turned to face me, her eyes dark.

"I have to go to them," she said. The moment the words left her mouth, my hand shot up to grab her wrist. There could only be two outcomes to this story, but abandoned alone in a hospital infested with zombies definitely felt like the lesser of two evils, the other being a lab rat and all. Still, the thought of being left on my own hit me like a sledgehammer. My throat constricted, and I couldn't get air into my lungs.

"If they search this place, they will find you. They won't if I'll go to them." I sensed the urgency in

Angie's voice.

Unable to speak, I nodded. I wanted her to know I understood even though it scared the shit out of me.

"You know what will happen if they take you, and I don't want that, but I can't promise you I'll come back or find you again," she said. "I will try. God knows I will try, but I can't promise." Her voice broke.

It wasn't what I wanted to hear. I wanted her to promise she'd come back for me, to rescue me from this place, although I appreciated her honesty. I'd feel pretty crappy about it if I sat here waiting for her and she never showed.

"I understand," I managed to say and tightened my grip on her wrist. "Still, I'd rather die here than on an examination table." Angie's eyes went wide.

"That's not going to happen," she said without the conviction I had hoped for. She started to explain that the evacuation of the building would start soon enough. Rescue teams were already scheduled to get the rest of the patients out the day after the military had cleared out the cancer ward. They probably hadn't expected the hospital to be overrun with zombies, but that wouldn't stop them from coming.

We had been running or rolling around this hospital for almost a day, and they shouldn't be long. Angie told me that because the ground and second floor were crowded with infected, the rescue teams might send assault teams by helicopter first—to carve out a route to evacuate the remaining patients.

I could tell she was trying to reassure me, trying to

get me to go with the rescue teams, but something told me she wasn't sure it was the best thing for me to do.

"You can pretend to belong to another ward," she said. "They'll take you to a safe place."

I snorted a sorrowful laugh and rubbed a hand over the pitiful amount of hair on my head.

"As if they'd mistake me for anything I'm not," I said and felt my voice break. My shoulders lifted then slumped.

"Don't be stupid, ki—" she started to say but swallowed the word. The loud, metallic voice boomed across the hall. Angie jumped to her feet at the sound. She hesitated, exchanging glances between the bathroom door and me.

"I have to go," she said, attempting a matter-of-fact tone that didn't come fully across. Forcing a straight face, I nodded. I wanted to appear strong, if only to reassure her that I would be all right.

She cursed as the metallic voice called out her name and rank and then looked at me with a pained look. She raised her fist. "Till we meet again."

I raised my fist and held it to hers.

"Next time."

Just like that, she was gone. I could hear the muffled exchange of words down the hall, but couldn't make any sense of them. Later, I heard the rotor blades cut through the air, and then everything returned to screams of the dying and moans of the zombies.

11

It felt like an agonizingly long time, waiting in that stupid bathtub, and without a watch, I had no way of telling how much time had passed. After a while, I heard footsteps running up and down the hall along with voices and the sound of people scrambling along. Someone entered the room, but I hid under the blankets and shower curtain. I couldn't do it. I couldn't announce myself to the evacuation team. I was too afraid these rescuers might be part of whatever Angie had been part of. Shivering like a baby, I hid until the sound of footsteps in the hall faded and disappeared.

Fear ripped through me at the thought of leaving the bathroom or this tub. I even kept drawing out the times I used the toilet. Besides, there was a drain in the tub. As long as I stayed on one side, peeing wasn't a problem.

It wasn't the zombies I feared. I knew they wouldn't touch me. Everything else scared the shit out of me. I finally understood Angie's struggle with leaving me behind. Had she thought I would die out here on my own? I started to think she might have been right, but at least, there wouldn't be any poking and prodding.

I slept most of my second day in the bathtub. When the last strip of sunlight had faded from the room adjacent to the bathroom, I couldn't ignore my stomach's cries for food any longer. The last time I had eaten was the night before Chuck showed up at my bedside. Adrenaline had kept me going the entire day as we ran from the zombies. Fear of discovery had kept me frozen in place for most of the day after.

The packet Angie had dropped into the bathtub turned out to be an MRE—a Meal Ready to Eat. It wasn't much, but then, I guess she hadn't expected me to stay. She'd thought I'd leave with the rescue crews. It hadn't been enough to soothe the hunger that had built for almost two days.

The agonizing process of climbing out of the tub and onto my new mad-scientist wheelchair had left me exhausted. Even then, the chair kept fighting me. It felt as if the brakes had remained clamped onto the wheels, and there was a squeaky sound every time I made a turn. It made the trip down the hall difficult. In their effort to get Angie and the remaining patients out, the soldiers had, I guessed, killed many of the zombies roaming this floor. Considering I had to wheel around their bodies, I would have preferred moving ones.

The hall looked nothing like the pristinely cleaned hallway that belonged in a hospital. The smell of death and decay hung in the air. Blood spatters in all forms and sizes covered the walls and floors. Bodies littered the linoleum. In some places, bodies lay in stacks where the soldiers must have piled them on top of each other. For some, only their clothes told me something of the story of whom they must have been, a doctor, a nurse, a soldier, but for most, nothing would reveal their identity ever again. The hospital had been evacuated, and I didn't expect anyone would set foot in here for a while. It made me wonder how long these bodies would lie scattered across these floors or how long zombies would roam these halls. When it came to the thought whether I would be one of them, I shoved it from my head.

I used the elevator to reach the ground floor. The main restaurant was on that floor, and I wanted to see whether I could find some food. The vending machines were my last resort, but that would mean I had to break them open somehow.

The ground floor looked to be a lot more crowded. Zombies shuffled the halls without purpose. I guessed that for as long they couldn't detect anything tasty to nosh on, they didn't know what to do with themselves. The reassurance I felt about wanting to die here instead of on an examination table wasn't as strong as before. Dread filled the emptiness left by the lack of food in my stomach. The hunger inside faded.

Forcing my chair between the bodies of the dead and undead, I caught sight of one of the restaurant entryways. It wouldn't do me any good to go in that way. There wouldn't be any access to the kitchen with this chair, but I had a way around that.

One of the cooks, a friendly, chubby guy who'd looked like Swedish Chef from *The Muppet Show*, had given me a tour once. He had shown me around the kitchen with its massive pots and miles of stainless steel tables. He had shown me an alternative entry.

The employee's entry doors stood open, and I felt glad. They looked like a pain in the butt to open. With a little effort, I managed to roll the chair past the threshold.

My head barely reached above the tables as I rolled past them. Something smelled funky, and I saw the lights on an oven still lit up. The kitchen felt strangely empty and looked, for the most part, untouched. Past the food displays on the other side of the counter, I could see a couple of zombies that milled around the restaurant tables. They didn't even seem to notice me. Then a fluid motion pulled my attention, and I froze. Zombies had lost their ability to move like that. My gaze shifted to the zombies milling in the restaurant. Nothing had disturbed them.

My heart lifted with the smile on my face. It had to be Angie; who else would be able to stroll past those zombies? She had come back for me, hadn't she? Not wanting to be an idiot, I kept my mouth from shouting her name. In an attempt to keep the squeaking to a minimum, I rolled my chair past the tables. Someone stood at the pantry door. My heart pounded like crazy at the possibility that Angie had come for me, but the lack of military clothing made my heart sink. She wore cargo pants and a black jacket, but it wasn't Angie.

I stared at the figure of a woman. She stood in front of the pantry door, and there was clearly something inside. One of her hands held a gun, and the other hovered over the door handle. It seemed as if she debated whether to enter or not. I stared at her in awe: she was so tall. I realized that from my position, probably everyone looked tall, but I'd bet she could rival that tall, dark lieutenant with those brilliant jade eyes I had seen with Angie. Despite her too-skinny frame, she looked like a freaking amazon, but with very short fuzzy hair like mine. It seemed I had discovered the reason she was able to move past the zombies without effort. For a moment, I debated whether I should show myself to her. She didn't look like a serial killer, although she did carry a gun. The blood on her cargo pants and the bandages on her face told me she hadn't come out unscathed, which could explain the gun. However, she had a friendly face, and I decided to risk it.

"What's up?" I said.

I didn't expect her to shoot at me.

Find out what happens next!!
in

Brooklyn, Wheels and Zombies

The next book in the Wheels and Zombies series
by
M. Van

Ash

A novella in the
Wheels and Zombies series
M. Van

Thanks for picking up this book and I hope you've
enjoyed it. I would really appreciate it if you left a
review.

If you would like to find out more,
visit www.42links.net and join the mailing list.